PRACTICAL TALES FOR CHILDREN

AND OTHER STORIES

BY

MARK ROMYN

EXIT PRESS
SAN FRANCISCO

Cover drawing by Michelle Talgarow
Back cover photo by Brian Shimetz
Book design by Richard Livingston

First Edition: January 2012

Additional information about EXIT PRESS at www.theexit.org.

ISBN: 978-0-9843964-3-6

EXIT PRESS
156 Eddy Street
San Francisco, CA 94102-2708
mail@theexit.org

My sincere thanks to Christina Augello and Richard Livingston of EXIT Theatre for all their good ideas and hard work. Without those two this book would still be in that pile of dreams. I would also like to thank all my friends and family for reading and encouraging my writing over the years. Special appreciation to Martha Steele for her copy edit job.

CONTENTS

Introduction vii

Author's Note ix

The Man-Made Man 1

The Horror of Hofbrau House 5

Baby 11

Afterlife 13

Billy 25

Infection in 84 29

Haunted House-Sitting 35

James Bond vs. Santa 37

Easy Going 47

Space Pants 49

Practical Tales for Children . . . 53

Making Friends 61

The Last Wish 67

Lost and Found 71

The Illustrated Tom 75

The Hatching 79

Mirror Man 83

Duncan's Diagnosis 87

Time Travelers 91

Looking For Love 95

Like Yesterday 99

INTRODUCTION

There's no one better at taking a reader to horror and no one better at making them giggle while there. Mark Romyn mischievously leaps into the arms of the living dead. He dares to tell any creepy truth, and even the faint of heart, like me, become liberated reading his chilling description of our absurd world and then grateful for the way he has made us laugh.

Not long ago, on a lunch break in the middle of the financial district, I nervously sipped tea. Small among the skyscrapers, I watched people race to catch a bus or crowd themselves into various lunch crevices, eating fast to get back to the grind, frowns on most of the faces. I wanted just a little time to be something entirely different. To leave this rat race and just go away. To crawl out of this slave's skin. An eerie fear scuttled up my spine, and I felt a nausea one of any of Romyn's characters might feel. After all, his horror is fantastic but keenly accurate.

I tried to shift my thoughts to ease the pain. There might be things I could do, think, or eat that could stave off this anxiety attack.

In our world we have many folks trying to sooth us. Public television, once commercial free, now offers up Wayne Dyer, Suze Orman, Deepak Chopra, and brain fitness, along with the occasional advertisement for cars. There's a particular free newsprint publication that displays various workshops, retreats, and spiritual diva headshots worthy of Hollywood. Sometimes I'll repeat a Deepak mantra or plan a brain-fitness meal to stave off a little terror.

But my heart beat louder and faster, and it looked like the anxiety attack would seize the entire workday. Until I remembered "James Bond vs. Santa. "

It's difficult to feel any pain while riding that story's wave of tasty, sex-spoofed fancy. However, even his most fanciful entertaining stories pack an insightful whack. There are many writers who tackle death, memory, conformity, stupidity, but not with such humorous irreverence.

It's also difficult for me to strike the balance between distant literary criticism and personal experience. That said, I'll take the personal: Romyn's stories are my friends. Good friends who don't lie. They outline the grotesque life trap, but they'll reach out to hold my hand, give a squeeze, and then a welcomed, witty wink. In the wild sci-fi, in the hilarious horror, I find no superficial tonic. I find a story as difficult as life and thankfully, wickedly funny.

Cameron Galloway

AUTHOR'S NOTE

While selecting stories to appear in this book, I engaged in a bit of time travel. I traveled back to the year 1989, the year that *Afterlife* was written. I felt the emotions and concerns I had twenty-two years ago. Each story I read was in itself a condensed packet of my personality from a different time. Fortunately my life hasn't been all that bad, so these trips weren't too unpleasant. But being a person who prefers to look forward rather than backward, this process of life review became somewhat of a chore.

And as I reviewed these works of mine, I became nagged by terrifying thoughts, "Were these stories any good? Was I a hack? Would readers shake their heads, groan, and toss the book aside?"

I realized that the intensity of my self-doubt was directly affected by my mood. If tired and beaten-down by the dramas of daily life, my stories were the trifling squeaks of a talentless ego seeking validation. If in a good mood, I perceived my stories as works that were fun and fine—happy things to share with a world of eager readers. So, like a child that plays upon its parent's moods to achieve its desires, I learned to approach my works only when Daddy Brain was feeling good and generous.

It has taken five years to select and edit these short stores to fill this slender book, so you can see just how often Daddy Brain was in the right mood.

Today I am feeling good and generous, and I offer this collection to you with pride. It is my sincere desire that you are feeling good and generous today too!

Mark Romyn

P.S.: Not all of my stories in this collection involved a great deal of "time travel," some are fresh and new, as I continue to write. I am writing now!

THE MAN-MADE MAN

Rolo Frankenstein had many passions, one of which was to create life. As a child he loved to dismember squirrels and put them together again. Bodies were three-dimensional jigsaw puzzles, as Rolo saw it, and puzzles were fun. . . . The adult male body that lay before him today was a completed puzzle; that in itself gave him joy. However, it was a dead puzzle, and that would have to change.

All the tools of the laboratory bubbled, sparked, and smoked. The big wheels were cranked. The switches were thrown. The body lay face-down on a table, a crown of electrodes on its head. The body convulsed and jerked and a smell of burnt hair pervaded the lab. Rolo switched off the machinery, walked briskly to his creation, and jabbed a hypodermic into its ass. The created moaned.

"It's alive," thought Rolo. He then petted the newborn man's hair, checked its pulse, and secured its leather bindings. He bent over the creature . . . whispered, "Your name is Barry," and tiptoed away.

"You must be very proud of yourself," said Nancy Frankenstein as she dropped her nightgown and lay on the bed. Rolo smiled at his wife and said, "I am." He removed his lab coat, dropped his nightgown, and joined her on the bed. "Science is proud of me also," he said softly. "We have entered a new beginning, a new age. My discovery, pulled from the womb of thought, spanked by empirical study, now cries for development and marketing. I will call upon your brother tomorrow, my dear. No doubt he will see the immense opportunity for profit."

A smile grew upon Nancy's face, "Oh darling," she said, "I smell MONEY."

Before going to sleep the couple fornicated.

* * *

Bob Schmidt, the world-famous entrepreneur, faced his brother-in-law and shook his head . . . the fool had brought a monster into his office. He asked his brother to sit down. The monster was ushered to a corner, where it stood looking sheepish. "I suppose you made it yourself," said Schmidt.

The scientist beamed, "Yes I have. I did it all by myself, using found materials. I have the cost breakdown with me." He then added, "I have created life . . . and it is cost effective."

A piece of paper exchanged hands.

Schmidt gave the cost analysis a cursory glance and said, "It works?"

"Completely functional."

"Is it super strong?"

"No."

"Is it super intelligent?"

"No."

"Can it do data entry?"

The monster stepped forward and stretched out its arms. "I am a Human Being," it implored in a squeaky voice.

The two men smiled.

Bob Schmidt snorted a short cynical laugh into his hand and said, "Did you train him to say that?"

Rolo Frankenstein grinned broadly. "Yes, yes I did," he admitted.

The Monster lowered its arms and returned to its corner. "I'm a cleaning monster!" it squeaked. It then tried to smile.

"Sssh! Now, now!" the scientist ordered with a snap of finger.

The men shared a quiet moment of reassessment and tactic.

"It's awfully ugly . . . will those stitches come out?" began Schmidt.

"Some will," said Frankenstein, "but these are the 2030s, a few scars and stitches won't bother anyone; if anything, the 'monster look' might be considered a fashion statement."

Schmidt leaned back in his chair and took a long, deep breath. "Obviously, it's easy to train. . . . What's the life expectancy?'

"Well, I haven't been able to do a longitudinal study as of yet. But I would assume thirty, forty years."

Schmidt nodded, glanced at the creature, and said, "All right Rolo, this is what we're gonna do. . . ."

* * *

Rolo Frankenstein was disappointed. He would not become the second wealthiest man in the world. His brother-in-law had suggested putting a few demo-models in circulation and then selling the patent quickly. Schmidt thought that The Monster concept had no "legs," and that it violated the basic rule of commerce: The Rule of Supply and Demand. And Rolo knew his brother was right. This was the 2030s, and with eight billion people on this planet—who needed more—who would pay for more? His creature had a highly perceived value in the consumer's mind at the moment. But the moment was fleeting, and the consumers' perception was based on faulty judgment. The world's inventory of humanity was overstocked. His creation was a novelty at best.

The creature was sold to a nightclub as a bartender. He made drinks well and saved his tips. He married and had a child. He outlived his creator. He bought a small bar in a quiet town. When folks made fun of him, he'd say, "Fuck off."

THE HORROR OF HOFBRAU HOUSE

Under a broken, obscured, and forgotten bridge of stone in a small town in Germany . . . a troll slept. He breathed in and out slowly, as he had done for drowsy centuries. He had become like his bridge, an object that existed but was now invisible—a ghost of an inconsequential memory long lost. The troll slept and did not shift or stir. But today, this cold October day, he would awaken. And naturally, he would wake up hungry....

"Udo! What are you doing?" said Inge Heinz in German.

The pudgy, eight-year-old boy in shorts stood in the kitchen with his hands at his sides and slowly moved his tongue in his mouth. Udo was doing nothing.

Inge Heinz frowned, put her hands to her still shapely hips and said, "Go get your father from the Hofbrau House and tell him to come home right now! If he isn't home in twenty minutes, he'll get no dinner! The swine dog!" she said in German.

The large (but still little) boy silently obeyed his mother and grabbed his cap and moved to the door and opened it. Before exiting, he turned and looked up to his mother for something he knew he wouldn't get. Inge Heinz understood the boy's glance of need and it exasperated her. She had no love to give to this child, and there he was letting the cold air in.

"And don't come home without him!" she barked as she sent him off with a shove and a slam of door.

A few seconds later, Fritz Kaufman came up behind Inge Heinz and with both hands squeezed her breasts deeply as if the breasts were made of foam rubber. "So you want him home now, huh?" he said.

Inge Heinz groaned and said "I know my Husband. Now that I

have told him to come home—he won't." She turned into her lover's arms. "We have hours."

Now Inge Heinz could smile. . . .

A little finch fluffed up its feathers and blinked in the cold wind. The little bird born of spring was dying in fall. It was sick and starving—and now—it was dead. It fell from the swaying branch of rust-colored leaves. It fell upon the sleeping face of the troll. The troll opened its cobweb encrusted eyes, sat up, and stared at the dead bird that now lay in its lap.

The troll shook the dusty gravel from its head and fingered the spiders from its ears. It sneezed. It yawned. It stretched out its long, hairy, orangutan arms. It then popped the little bird into its mouth and crunched, savoring the warmth of the blood and tenderness of its soft bones. There was youth in the bird's body and some sorrow too—and the troll's favorite foods were young and sad things.

Of course, the troll preferred human children—they had a nice meat-to-fat ratio and were packed pies of emotion. You see, a child is not yet used to the disappointments of daily life and feels them acutely. A child may have its happy moments, but it also knows too well the shadows of loss, and tears, and powerlessness, and loneliness, and fear. And the troll—being a demon and a thoroughly evil thing—found sweetness in the meat of sorrow.

Our troll stood up and now became four-and-a-half feet tall. He looked at the ruins of his bridge, gazed at the dry, tree-filled river bed and surveyed the road that led to town. If he were to eat (and eat he must) he would have to leave this place and find a new spot to trick and devour children. He stuck his nose into the air and sniffed—and the hairs of his nose flew back like palm trees in a hurricane. He smelt children and one was near . . . on that road. The troll knocked the mud and dirt from his lederhosen, found his cap under a stump, spat out a feather, and took to the road. The demon began to whistle a polka.

Young Udo thought "Why does she do this to me? Why does she make me go and try and get him? It just only makes him mad. Oh, and I'm so hungry and it's so cold." He moved his fat little legs faster. His cheeks began to redden in the chill. "Oh, I'm cold and hungry and it's getting dark," thought the boy.

The Hofbrau House was now in the boy's sight, and Udo's mind turned to its wonders: It wasn't really that bad a place; there were sausages inside and potato pancakes with applesauce and the banisters that led down to the bathrooms were fun to play on and there were lots of things to look at and you could run around the big place and no one bothered you much and Dad would be drunk and happy—maybe. He picked up the pace, and being a chubby boy, he began to sweat.

The troll smelled the boy—smelled the tears in his sweat and the candy-coated fear in his breath. The demon ached and starved for the child's flesh. Drool poured from the monster's lips and over its chin like milk from a pitcher. The quickly waddling boy came under the sight of the troll. And although it was out of character for the troll to enter the town, the monster was driven beyond its control by its hunger lust. It stretched out its obscene, six-inch tongue that swung and pointed like a weather vane in the direction of the boy's neck. The troll clenched its hands slowly and then opened them, and then it began to run.

Little Udo turned to look behind him and saw something out of a fairy tale at the end of the block. The thing was so very scary and it was moving so very fast—so very fast! It was as if his own hand had been stretched away to a blocks distance, but now had been pulled right up to his face, taking the monster along with it. And there it was—looking at him—breathing on him—right smack in his face! Udo screamed and threw himself against the door of the Hofbrau House just as he felt the fingers of the monster poke into the fat of his lower back. The door swung open. . . .

Before the troll an enormous room teaming with men and bustling with women carrying steins and platters of food . . . loud voices and polka music . . . smoke and animal heads . . . tables and benches filled with men and food and drink and even more men. The troll was stunned, and, as it loosened its grip, the boy wriggled away.

A big, square woman with straw-colored hair walked up to the troll, held up a finger and said "One? Right this way." She grabbed him by the arm and led him along rows of shouting, drunken men sitting thigh to thigh on benches and swinging steins of beer larger than their bony heads—men trying to sing, eat, and drink simultaneously. She dropped him down on a bench in the midst of these men. She then took away the empty glass before him and wiped the surface of the wet wooden table with an equally wet rag. "Light or dark?" she said. The troll was bewildered and did not answer. "Light," she answered for him and moved away.

For a moment, the troll felt as out of place and as small as a cat turd in a cathedral. But then he remembered who he was and took the place in. . . .

To the troll's right, a big-headed man whose face was a shattered mirror of blood-red, broken capillaries, shouted in a dialect that no one understood and gulped beer. To the troll's left, a man dressed in black wool slept, his bloated face shiny with sweat. And there before the sleeping man lay a platter of sausages. . . .

The troll, on impulse, snatched a white sausage and crammed it into his mouth. He tore into the soft meat with his sharp shark teeth—and then it happened—a rush of pleasure so expansive, so overwhelming, so soul-stuffing-bursting—that he ejaculated into the leather of his pants. There was youth in the meat, and such, such wonderful suffering. To have such pain-infused meat the baby animal must have been tortured! The troll smacked his lips and looked at the slow, dull faces around him. "Could these men have made this delicacy?" he wondered. "But how could mortals create or even dream of the blessings of my foods—unless. . . ?" Perhaps there was one of his kind in the kitchen. He would have to check later.

A woman with breasts the size of piglets dropped a stein of beer in front of the troll. The troll grabbed another white sausage and excitedly waved it in her face.

"You want the bockwurst?"

"Yes! Yes!" shouted the troll.

The woman smiled and, a minute later, arrived with a platter the size of a dishrack heaped with the bone-white sausages.

The troll grabbed her arm and pleaded earnestly "What, what is this?"

The woman wiped the sweat from her eyes and said with fatigue, "They are sausages made with the meat of veal . . . the young calf. It's very tender—very good." She then looked at the ugly dwarf a little closer and said "They cost eight euros."

The troll said "I would give you all the gold from my cave for this. But. . . ." And in the flash of a bumblebee's wing, the demon snatched the sleeping man's wallet. "But," continued the troll smoothly, "I can give you . . . euros."

The theft went unnoticed and the waitress was appeased.

And now to the tasty sausages! The troll fell into them, ripped them with his broken-glass teeth, felt the hot grease splash his throat. The sensations of the warm, soft flesh slipping past the tongue, down the gullet, and into the stomach made him giddy. The beer was good too, not as thick as blood, but satisfying. The troll's hunger began to abate, and he felt so good that he began to dance in his chair to the polka. He liked this place! He felt comfortable here, in this, this "Hofbrau House."

A shadow fell upon the troll, and he looked up into the face of a big German standing before him. The little child he had chased nudged the leg of the big German like a baby elephant seeking comfort from its larger kin.

"My son says that you scared him."

The troll smiled (without showing his teeth) and raised his glass to the big man.

The father laughed and cuffed his son. "You see Udo, he's just an old man. A little old man. He is ugly. But not as ugly as some. My name's Karl Heinz. Will you let me buy you a beer?"

The troll nodded and waved him over. The father shoved aside the sleeping man and sat next to the troll.

"I haven't seen you before, are you new to our town?"

The troll replied "I like this place. I am going to live here."

"You like our Hofbrau House—I can tell."

"Yes, I am going to live here."

"That's great," said Karl Heinz with a laugh, "I live in this place too! Just about!"

The troll laughed good-naturedly and looked at the cowering child. "And what about your son—shouldn't he be at home with his mother?" he said with a hint of teeth in his smile.

The Father swung his head down to glare at the boy, then flipped his face back up with a smile and rumpled the boy's hair. "No, he can wait," he said with a careless laugh.

"Yes," said the troll, mimicking the laugh, "he can wait." The troll bit into a sausage. "He can wait," he repeated softly.

BABY

I guess, I'm like any other expectant father—I'm nervous as hell! My wife (God bless her) is just a few yards away in the delivery room giving birth to our son. I was supposed to be in there with her, but at the last minute, I felt a panic attack coming on and backed out. I feel quite ashamed. I mean, what modern man isn't in the delivery room with his wife nowadays? We had even taken all the classes together to prepare for this day. But I wouldn't have been any help to her today. A man has to know his limitations. And the wife certainly knows mine. She let me off the hook. If there are any resentments she'll let me know, and I certainly will make the amends. But then again, without me she wouldn't be there in the first place. It was my job status, projected income, life expectancy, and security rating that got us this blessing.

Oh! I think I heard a baby cry! What a strange, marvelous sound. What a rare gift to hear it. That wouldn't be Cayenne's baby. (Cayenne is my wife's name.) She can't have a human baby—only the most genetically sound can do that. Yeah, that ole cancer bug runs in her family. Her GPO indicates that she'll get breast cancer in the next twenty years or so. She'll be cured of course, but drugs and treatment are expensive, and a pretty hefty chunk of our paychecks goes straight into her cancer reserve. However, like so many young married couples, we still wanted a child. It's only natural. And we wanted to be good citizens and, of course, please God. As the President says, " You can't have Family Values . . . without a family."

We applied for project "Puppy Love" and again, thanks to me mostly, got the go ahead from the State Department of Family.

I'll never forget the day Cayenne came home from the Pregnancy Center. She was ecstatic! She had just been implanted. She had new life growing in her, and she was so proud, so happy. She pulled me to the prayer corner and together that night we poured out such thanks to the Almighty. We praised the Lord for guiding the hand of science and government. We praised the Lord for opening the eyes of man to the true love of life and creation. And we gave thanks to the President, who took sixty-year old technology—and had the wisdom and faith to develop it—so that we could receive the blessings of parenthood! Bless you Sir!

Cayenne and I loved her pregnancy. We spent many delightful hours coming up with names for the baby and setting up the nursery. When we found out that Cayenne was going to have a boy beagle, we decided (finally) upon the name of "Douglas," after my grandfather. Our boy's full name will be "Douglas Allen Thompson." Sounds rather distinguished . . . don't you think?

Of course, we know and accept all the responsibilities of having a child: love, education, vaccinations, spaying, grooming, diet, and exercise. Cayenne is going to take a leave from work for six months to be with the baby during the all-important formative months. Also, we will have to face the burden of outliving our child . . . something that has put off many from having dog or cat children. But we are not going to deny ourselves the joys of life just because the flesh is impermanent and must die in order to reach eternal salvation. And we will face our beagle boy's death, secure in the knowledge that he will be received by the Lord. And that we will see him again some blessed day!

But onto happier thoughts. Yesterday, I tried on the Breast Vest, and boy did the wife and I have a laugh. We will share in the breast-feeding duties as any modern couple would. Still the vest looked funny on me—and strangely sexy—God forgive!

Oh my goodness, a nurse is before me. It's time to see my child!

There's the wife on the bed—her eyes bright, her skin flushed. I've never seen her so beautiful. My baby is being handed to me. He's so, so very tiny, and wet, and his face is so wrinkled and small. He's perfect and he's mine. Oh my God, my son just licked my nose. This is the happiest day of my life.

Afterlife

Chapter One

The metallic tube shot through the black concrete tunnel. Early morning commuters sat fatly in their chill clothes, bland sleep-eyed discomfort easing from their tired faces. The lights were too bright. The people rocked meatily mindless. No one spoke. No one smiled. Some read. Some stared. Everyone going someplace else—wishing they were someplace else. A routine. A routine that B. Holtz had at first hated and now accepted and now would almost defend.

Holtz felt a light skittering on the back of his neck and slapped away at the movement. "A fly?! Oh my god, it was! How repulsive," came the thoughts. The young businesswoman to his right glared at him with open distaste. Holtz stared back at the young businesswoman and quickly thought, "God, she looks terrible," before embarrassedly turning toward the window. The fly returned to his hand. It looked to Holtz, in his sleep-deprived mind, like a black cutout moving in jumpy stop-animation. His right hand came down hard and fast, and when he lifted it, a black and yellow mush lay twitching on his flesh. He squirmed effeminately and nervously flicked away the wet crumples of body. He then stared at the glass window, wiped the dead moisture off on his pants, and wondered why the stupid fly didn't move faster.

To Holtz's left, moving slowly and smoothly, came the local 34th Street exit. Commuters of all typical types stood or sat. They all looked particularly bad today: pale, sweaty, work-beaten. But all this was tolerably normal. What struck Holtz (what honestly moved him) was the sight of this eleven-year-old boy—this eleven-year-old boy standing barefoot in his yellow pajamas with his bright, tearstained face animatedly flexing and puckering. The boy screeched terror and sadness and death. The boy was crying and reaching and beating. And all around him stood a mortuary calm of commuters. Holtz wanted to get up, to actually stand and leave and do something, but his impulse was snuffed as the moving train slipped into the blackness of tunnel.

Holtz rode his train home early that day. The entire city had been let out early in order to observe a funeral. Holtz sat miserably in his train and tried to cry, but found it physically impossible—nearly all the basic attributes and functions of having a living body had been found to be physically impossible. Preposterously enough, everyone's bodies no longer lived—movement, vision, and thought were possible—basic life functions were not. What caused humanity's hearts to thump off and why animation and cognizance continued after death were mysteries, but the unmistakable, undeniable, moronically sci-fi comic book truth of it all was that mankind was dead and yet walked the earth.

When Holtz left his train, he went straight home. Once in the sanctity of his quiet home, Holtz took off his coat and tie, made his coffee, and lit his cigarette. He then watched his coffee get cold and his cigarette burn. He clicked on the TV. Anchorperson Sylvia Chance was on, mouthing words vacant of breath, a subtitle train rolling below. Words normally incongruous were now bizarrely jigsawed together . . . "Purification Center, Mass Suicide Failure, Self-Embalming Kit, Projected Animation Deadline, Problems of No Growth Infancy. . . ."

Holtz turned off his television. He stared at his moist, gray, vein-swollen arms and hands and then slowly walked towards the bathroom mirror.

"It's not that bad. It's still me. That's me. Hey, it could be worse . . . all right," said Holtz to the blue-gray Holtz in the mirror.

He pulled a small shaving band-aid off his jaw and checked the droplet of scab beneath.

"It'll never heal," he thought. "This, this . . . this right now will be the best I'll ever look. From this moment on, everything will go downhill." Holtz's eyes met his own reflected gaze and a strange sad resolve came upon him.

Upside-down feet slipped through a homespun harness, legs

snaked after, and leather creaked to accept the weight. A white plastic scalpel was drawn across the carotid and jugular. Dark, dark brown blood flushed out the wound over a tightly grimaced face and down the bathroom drain. The nude, dead body hung suspended alone in its own bathroom until the blood finally stopped shooting, pouring, trickling, dribbling, and plop, plop, plopping. Now it was time to get upright, slip in one's own juices and attach the latex embalming aerosol to the appropriate orifice. A whiz and a hiss, a quick inflation, a sudden reflex vomit of plastic (which science could not explain) and it was all over. Only the flesh-toned adhesive tape need be applied to the incision marks and the insecticide defogger turned on. After twenty minutes of standing nude in goggles, it would be time to wash that blood right out of your hair and enjoy a long shower. . . . Holtz did it all himself, and afterwards felt a little better, a little cleaner. He then dressed quickly and decided to go visit a nearby friend, for naturally he had much he wanted to say and share.

"Hearing Out of Order—Door Is Open"

Holtz chuckled to himself and entered the home of his friend, Matt Browner. He found Matt seated in front of his television set, an idle drink and cigarette before him. "Hey Matt, how ya doin'?" said Holtz with silent lips, before damning himself for the fortieth time with the realization that he was unable to speak. Matt, however, was ready. He picked up a card that read "HI," then another that read, "Sit down and stop looking stupid," then another that read, "I've been writing these dumb cards all afternoon—makes me realize what a horrible conversationalist I am." Holtz laughed without vibration and eagerly grabbed a nearby and convenient pen and notepad. He started to write but stopped to stare into the face of his friend. Matt looked dead to Holtz, yet his eyes and face still gave off the light of friendly intelligence and good humor that Holtz loved him for. Holtz smiled in appreciation and Matt smiled back. Together they wrote a script.

"How do I look?"

"Like fly-food."

"I just embalmed myself."

"Pretty."

"Aren't you going to?"

"Yeah, I guess--my PUTREFACTION CENTER ran out of kits. I don't think I could do it though."

"Maybe Carla would do it for you."

"AMAZING how quick they set up those PUTREFACTION CENTERS, isn't it?"

"That's the way I like my society—well organized."

"No really, they must have known."

"I know. It's scandal time."

"Fuck scandal!!!"

"Someone's got to pay."

"We'll never find out who's responsible—massive fuck-ups like these are too embarrassing. No one wants to know."

"I do."

"Not everyone is dead."

"I know. I saw a live one this morning. It was sad."

"They say that two percent of the world's population is still alive. Pretty good percentages there, eh?"

"Right. I'm supposed to go back to work tomorrow."

"Me too."

"Are you?"

"I'm going to call in sick."

"HA HA."

"We're handling life-after-death pretty well, don't you think?"

"Not really, Matt."

"I know. God, I'm dying for a DRINK!!!"

"Me too."

"Damn it! What are we going to do?"

"Just go on living."

"YEAH, LIVING AND LIVING AND LIVING AND LIVING AND LIVING AND LIVING AND LIVING."

"Well, maybe tomorrow we'll wake up and really be dead—I'm confused."

"Ditto."

"I wish I could smoke."

"Me too."

"Matt, I'm tired of writing."

"Me too."

The two friends sat facing each other, looking awkward for a full minute. Holtz began a fumbling search of all his pockets for cigarettes as Matt smiled on sarcastically. Holtz gave up his quest and reached for that pack on the coffee table. He picked up that pack, stared at it, and gently put it back in the exact spot. He then smiled at his friend, arched his eyebrows, got up, and started towards the door. Matt got up to escort his friend. The "Well, I'll see ya arounds" and the "Maybe we can get together on Thursdays" were dropped and replaced by the silent formalities of handshakes, pats on the shoulders, and waves.

By the time Holtz found himself alone on the street, it had begun to rain. He thought, "I don't know if I'm going to be able to take this shit." He watched the city's cars lurch and hiccup their way along the street, as dead drivers became students of driving with unfeeling feet. "I don't think it's going to work," came the thoughts. It began to rain hard. "How weird it is—walking in the rain, feeling no urge to hurry—no urge to hunch the shoulders and scurry for shelter."

Most of the stores and restaurants around Holtz were closed and many had been vandalized or looted. "I don't know . . . I don't know. I don't think it's going to work," thought Holtz.

Chapter Two

The square held three hundred dead people and more were crowding in. Most of the dead people had not seen their own faces for a long time; black hoods and slits held the common countenance. Some of the less decayed decorated themselves with purposeful, artistic mutilations (the attachable human ear hanging from the right nipple, etc.). All the dead walked barefoot, for no old-fashioned flat shoe could ever contain their constantly gnarling feet. The dead hobbled, hopped, and slithered onto the large stone square, each carrying an orange ticket.

In the center of the square, rising above the mob, a large banner reading "MOBI LOTTO TODAY" flapped regularly. Beneath the banner, surrounded by many colorful flags and pennants, stood a wooden platform. Upon the platform, six live humans held electric wheelchairs over their heads. Each wheelchair had a large white number painted on it. Each wheelchair held the promise of months and months of extended mobility to the dead. The excited mob pushed forward, causing the air to be filled with the pop-clicks of soft bones and soft bodies being broken. The living humans, high above the mob, exchanged Cheshire smiles.

Holtz was a quarter mile away, swaying forward, draped in black. "Fuck the Lotto," he thought adamantly. "It's just a ruse. As if anyone really ever wins. Just a lot of ridiculous hope, misplaced faith. I don't understand the living," he continued to himself. "I mean, granted, they were very, uh, I guess, charitable to setup our new household, to replace order in our broken society, give us our electricity—keep our TVs warm. Propaganda, rules, Lotto—I can understand all that. But what I don't understand is the all important WHY? We can't work very well—Christ, as a workforce we're negligible. We aren't pretty to look at. We're poor entertainers. The living don't seek us out for friendship, or for anything really. . . so why should they care enough about us to look after our welfare and RULE US?! To rule the Dead? Why? We're not going to last. Hell, we're dead meat! We're a health risk to the fools. And anyhow, even if they could get us. . . ."

Holtz's oft-repeated thoughts were broken short by a rampaging 225-pound nude uniped. The living carrion was moving far too fast for its state of decay (large pieces were flying). "Aw Christ—watch it!!" screamed Holtz in vacuum voice. But the bounding, one-legged dead man's eyes rolled illogically as he sprung directly toward Holtz. Holtz shuffled left, turned his shoulder, and was awarded a minimal bump. His clavicle, however, snapped and his right shoulder and arm dropped two inches. The springing, one-legged dead man flopped rapidly on his way never realizing his transgression. And Holtz— Holtz began to stagger home.

He rationalized, "It's OK Bob, you're all right. . . . Things change. . . . Don't worry. . . . Remember when your nose fell off? Life went on. . . . No one noticed. . . . No one cared. . . . You might as well get used to it. . . . You might as well get used to it and keep going, eh? Come on now, let's fuck the lotto and go home and— and do something nice for ourselves, eh? Fine." And thus thinking, Holtz wandered away from the square, thereby missing the riot and consequent napalming.

On his way home, Holtz approached the house of his old friend, Matt Browner. "Jeez, I wonder how ole Matt's doin?" thought Holtz. (Holtz hadn't seen Matt, or for that matter, any of his friends for months.) "The last time I saw Matt, he was wearing some silly cellophane body bag, 'Vacuum Packed For Freshness' he told me. He had been losing his eyesight too . . . god it was depressing. All he could do was complain about how his girlfriend left him because he had lost his looks. He really ought to have embalmed himself."

Holtz stood in front of his friend's doorway—the old "Hearing out of order" sign was still hanging—today Holtz found little humor in it. "Best see Matt while you still can," said the quiet voice of his mind. He found the door open and stepped in.

Holtz found Matt on the kitchen floor in a small alcove next to the refrigerator. He had been reduced to a cloaked lump the size of a laundry basket. Holtz pulled out one of his prepared greeting cards, lifted an edge of Matt's cloak, and extended his card into the woolen darkness. There was no response. Holtz pulled his card out—both his hand and the card were covered in a thick, caramel-colored fluid.

Holtz's stained hand caressed Matt's veiled carcass, until the carcass quivered, and the stained hand flew up to find its master's gaping mouth. "Oh Matt! Jesus Christ, Matt!" screamed his lips. The stained hand fell limp. "A conscious mind," his mind staggered, "Alive—suspended in dark styrofoam silence—no stimulus—no nothing—alone—and till when? Till there is what?" But his worst fear was of his friend's trapped thoughts.

Holtz turned away. It was then that he noticed the cylindrical shapes he knew to be fingers lying randomly in the corners of the room. Holtz counted seven. He then consciously straightened himself and left.

It was late when Holtz got home, but he made it before curfew. Once inside, he began his hygiene routine; it was dull, meticulous work, but it forced him to focus on the minute concrete, and it in a way calmed him. "One thing for sure, he said to himself as he pulled a shard of glass from his foot, "my right shoulder and arm are just about useless. I can still use the hand," he continued, as he dipped his feet into a bucket of cleaning solution, "I've still got two hands."

He stripped nude, walked into his bathroom, shut the door and put on his goggles. He truly hated this part of the routine because of the tedium—the standing for twenty minutes in the insect defogger. But the vision of red and gray worms boring through his flesh forced him to comply with the stricture. Holtz stood in the thick mist and saw nothing but blank cotton white and tried not to think—or most importantly—feel. And he was mostly successful today, although his lips would move to form the word "Shit" every five minutes or so. (Holtz knew he was doing it too, though he did not want to postulate on the reason why.)

After his hygiene routine, Holtz moved to the closet and fumbled through his old life's clothing until he found his favorite comfy robe. The old blue robe was thin and tattered, but Holtz at the moment did not need it for its protective warmth. He put it on because it relaxed him. He then moved to the living room for some TV entertainment.

A popular game show was on. The show featured terrific prizes, a wheel of chance, and beautiful people hardly touched by death's decay. The TV camera and Holtz focused in on one winning brunette contestant. She had skin and a nose and shapely lips. She could jump up and down. Her breasts were inflated with supple flesh. She flashed a smile and eagerly moved her thin hands. . . . Holtz felt an old brain center begin to flash arousal. He thought of the televised woman naked and himself naked—whole and strong. But he quickly squelched these thoughts, for he knew them to be frustrating and ultimately depressing. He decided to fixate on the unfairness of decay. "Look at em—why they're beautiful," he spat to himself. "Why you never see people like that—why most people are so fuckin' ugly they put bags over their shit bodies! I don't own a mirror—nobody does—except maybe those freaks! HAHA NYEAH NYEAH HAHA," he jeered as the brunette lost on the wheel of chance.

"And look at this prize," read the TV set. "A classic, fully functional, walk-in freezer unit! Adapted for home use, this ICY BOY freezer will guarantee years of cosmetic freshness and extended mobility. Walk in and Stay Fresh—ICY BOY! This prize is worth . . . $30,485!!"

"Who wants to live forever?" snarled Holtz to himself, "Matt certainly doesn't."

He turned away from the set out of boredom and stared out at the near-dark skyline. Holtz watched the tree articulate and wave its bulk in the apparently strong wind. A thin sliver of moon shone fluorescent white in the evening sky. Gray hills of cloud moved swiftly without purpose.

Holtz turned back to the television. The City Unit Supervisor was on. It was an Emergency Broadcast! War was being declared! All the Class Three Animate were to report tomorrow for enlistment. Failure to enlist would be cause for incineration.

Holtz naturally was at first stunned by the words of war. However, his interest quickly turned to the speaker: the City Unit Supervisor was alive! Holtz watched the living man's eyes blink, his lips open and close, his mouth wet with saliva. He saw the supervisor speak, pause and breathe, and speak and breathe again. Holtz watched in rapture as living hands turned cards with swift grace and efficiency, as a uniformed chest and shoulders filled and swelled with smooth air, as a full head of shining hair shook and twitched with the vibrancy of the speaker's words. The living man was filled to capacity with swift heated blood and cooling generous air. He was alive.

Holtz stared at the Living Thing with admiration tinged with real love. Then the image blinked off and was replaced by the dead game show. Holtz's eyes expanded at the cruel horror. The contestants looked hideous: Their skin seemed as if it was made of wet sand; their bodies like mangled driftwood; their expressions labored and nightmarishly slow; all had naked, deformed fists for feet. . . . Holtz squeezed his eyes shut and dashed for the television set. He blindly beat the set's dials with his body until the set turned dark and was off.

He then sat down and bowed his head and pretended to be truly dead. . . . But he could not stop the thoughts: "Why war? The living had united the world for the sake of their own survival. What would happen to those who were too decayed to fight? Would they be incinerated? What about Matt? A living tombstone—alive forever? Or once incinerated did the soul cease to think—feel? How could anyone truly know such subjective answers? I don't want to fight. I don't want to leave home. Why do the Living want us to fight? A clever genocide?!" The thoughts moved too fast to be contained in a rational sequence, thereby preventing any true conclusions to be made. "Intellectual bumper cars," rambled Holtz, as his mind became anxious for a slow. "Tomorrow . . . tomorrow," he said to himself in a soothing voice, "Tomorrow you can find the answers. You can wait. Just stop now . . . it's OK. . . . Hey you promised yourself something special tonight, Bob. . . . How about a nice cozy fire eh?"

Holtz eagerly looked to the fireplace. He would need more wood, but he knew where to get some. Building a fire was also illegal, but he figured he could get away with it tonight. "A fire—what a lovely idea!"

Holtz scrambled to his feet and moved towards the cellar. (There were some old crates down there that certainly could be sacrificed). He knew the door leading to the cellar stairs to be stuck—the wood swollen by the damp. So Holtz grabbed that doorknob with his good arm and yanked with all his strength. The door swung open instantly and popped his head. The air rang with the familiar pop-click of broken bone, and Holtz staggered and swayed. He then began to giggle and then outright laugh silently at his own slapstick. He saw himself as a cartoonish stick figure, indestructible, yet constantly being smashed by its oversized actions. It was the first time he had laughed in months. It felt good.

It had taken a lot more work than he had figured on, but there it was—flickering orange, yellow and red—the fire. Holtz sat in his old armchair, before the fire, and allowed himself a little pride in his accomplishment.

Outside, the wind was blowing up a gale. Holtz could see the tree nearly bent completely back, rise for a second, and then be beat back with gusty violence. In the living room everything was dim grainy orange shadow—snug and peaceful.

"It's a good thing you enjoy your own company, Bob," he said to himself with a half-smile, "otherwise you'd be a lonely man."

A log rolled over and the room was momentarily lit yellow. Holtz was quietly cheered by the light of the fire, although he could not feel its warmth.

"Tomorrow's another day," he murmured to himself.

BILLY

The wind whistled through the trees like a happy bird the day I met Billy. He had his foot caught in a trap. His eyes were filled with anger . . . and a little fear too. But I bent down low and whispered in his ear, "Take it easy little fella—take it easy," as I pulled back them cold, iron jaws of that trap. I bandaged his bloody, torn leg and his eyes changed—they became the eyes of a thankful child. He followed me home and became mine.

I collect animals. I like to call it making friends. I just feed 'em a little, and talk with 'em a little, and play with 'em a lot, and they stick around. They're my pals. Every morning we go swimming in the lake. We splash and swim and wrestle in that ole muddy water until it's time for me to go to work. Then my pals go back to the cabin I built and sun themselves and make friendly-like until I comes a home.

I've got a lot of friends: There's Harry the squirrel, and Bob the raccoon, and Barry the skunk, and Nigel the chipmunk, and Hamilton the crow, and Chuck the bobcat, and Randy the mule, and Chris the bear, and Paul the mountain lion, and now . . . Billy the badger. Billy's my first badger.

I've got some people friends too: There's ole Red Tongue (he's a Blackfoot Indian) and there's ole Cappy Smalls, who lives about five miles from me. They comes ta visit every month or so. And there's old Jacques Le Feute. He's a hermit, and a French pirate, and he's got a falcon named Queenie. We don't talk much.

Here's my story. The sun baked the air like an oven bakes black bread the day that ole Italian came inta the territory. He ran a traveling animal show that had a monkey and a camel—and other critters that were more normal. He said he wanted ta collect more animals ta train for his show. He wanted ta buy my friends. But I told him that money can't buy friendship and "No."

I did tell that ole Italian where he could catch a mountain lion. I told him he could keep his animals with me for safe keeping. He said "Ho-kay," and offen he went. When he got ta the spot I told him ta go to, I surprised him and hit him on the head with a shovel. I hit him again, and I hit him good until I was sure he'd never move again. I left him where he lay, so all my scavenger friends could have a good meal.

I named the monkey Tad—and the camel Richard.

But that's another story.

One night when the moon was as high and bright as one of those overhead electric lights, my buddies Red Tongue (he's a Blackfoot Indian) and Cappy Smalls were sitting up late round the fire talking. We did some drinking too. Cappy was telling us stories of war, and about his Commander Douglas, and about Commander Douglas's Big Day. Then Red Tongue challenged me ta an Indian leg wrestling match. Cappy stopped his story right quick and told us ta take offen our pants—which we did right quick.

We lay on our backs and hooked our legs together and proceeded to work our muscles agin each other. It was a tough fight. We must of lay in that dust sweatin' and a groaning by the fire fer hours. All my animal friends rooted me along . . . and I was about to win when this strange object that was sort of shaped like a cigar or a banana slug came a-rocketing out of the sky. It was big. It hovered over our heads and started to make weird liquid-like sounds. We all got scared and started to run—all in different directions.

I ran like a crazy man for a long time. I stopped when I could run no longer and leaned agin a tree. Then I heard a snap and felt a big pain in my right foot. I fell into the deep pot of blackness that has been called unconsciousness.

When I came to, I realized that I had caught my foot in a bear trap. I had lost a lot of my own blood. I felt woozy. Then I saw my ole pal Billy the badger. He sniffed and whiskered me fer a spell— then he made up his mind. He turned and ran away. I cried "Billy! Billy! Don't leave me!" But he did. I then slipped back into that pot of darkness.

When I awoke, my leg felt as if it were a log of wood on fire. But guess who was there? . . . Billy! Billy was there and he had gotten help. Billy had brought Tad the monkey. Now you may not know this but monkeys are strong. That monkey's long hairy arms could bust a bull's back. He grabbed that trap and had me outta there faster than you could say, "Tad's the best monkey on Blue Mountain!"

With Tad and Billy's help, I made it back ta the cabin. Then all my animal friends took care of me and they nursed me back ta health.

I never saw Red Tongue again. But Cappy Smalls was all right, and boy did he have a story to tell—all about strange men from Mars that had tentacles all over, and how he had strange instruments stuck all over himself, and how he scared them by whistling—but that's another story.

I'm going to end my story with some sadness and some gladness. I found out that Billy weren't a male. He had run off for a little while and had got himself pregnant—and had babies—that's how I found out. I thought of changing his name to "Lady" or "Lady Billy" or "Queenie" or something, but I just couldn't do it. It just doesn't seem right for an old bachelor like myself to be livin with a woman. So, I got a big stick and beat that badger until it ran away.

Now the gladness! I saved a little boy badger cub. I named him Russell.

INFECTION IN 84

At one hour and ten minutes past sunset, something that looked like a meteor slashed through the black-blue sky, provoking the teens on the beach to turn their faces to the heavens and cry, "Whoa" in amazement. The "meteor" slipped behind a dark hump of mountain and vanished. And the teens turned up the boom box and continued to party like it was 1984—because that was the year. And beer cans fitzed open, and the sexed-up teens sniffed at each other with jerking, anxious eyes.

On the other side of the mountain, Dr. Larry Seamons and his drinking partner, Hal Sloan, exited the car and slowly approached the steaming crater. Crickets and soft crunches of feet upon dried pine needles and the clacking of a burning shrub were the only sounds . . . until Hal Sloan slurred, "Look at . . . what the. . . ?"

For like a plant sprouting and growing to adulthood in quick, time-lapse photography, a monstrous alien spacecraft erected itself from the crater. It looked like the biggest rotten banana the two men had ever seen. They tilted their heads back as far as they could without falling backwards and stared at the banana thing with mouths open. It was as tall as the tallest skyscraper, or as "tall as God," as Dr. Larry Seamons would later say to reporters, as he clutched a warm, sand-encrusted beer and waved a cigarette to the sky.

A rip at the base of the spacecraft appeared and began to ooze grey gelatin. The tear grew and widened, until it became a sphere. The gelatin foamed fiercely from the orifice. And Dr. Larry Seamons turned and streaked away like a discovered house mouse.

Hal Sloan said, "I think we should get out of here" to the vacant space left by the good doctor, just as the aliens burst through the gelatin.

They were triangular in shape, had long, snake-like arms, and, instead of legs, had a single flesh wheel that provided unicycle mobility. The aliens, of course, were very big—the size of garbage trucks. And their heads looked like pinecones with hundreds of eyes attached. An obscene, pulsating pucker served as a mouth.

Yes, like Evel Knievel shooting through a paper hoop on his motorcycle, three aliens shot from out of the foam and skidded to a stop before Hal Sloan.

Hal had time to whimper and give the peace signal with a shaking hand before the lead alien grabbed him and swung him into the air. Hal was upended and his head was put to the monster's mouth. The alien popped open the top of Hal's head with its tongue and swigged down all the blood, fat, and soft tissue in a few gulps. The empty Hal container was thrown aside as the alien wiped its mouth on the back of its arm and said telepathically, "These free-range Humanoids taste a little gamey to me, but they're still good. Let's check this place out."

The aliens then roared down the mountain road—white exhaust trailing from their anus pipes.

Dr Larry Seamons kept running. He would have been amazed at his own stamina, if he hadn't been so afraid. He could have taken the car, or have run down the road, but the closeness of the trees made him feel more secure and safe in the primitive hiding sense. He was now an animal, being hunted by some big mean thing that meant to kill him—of this he was certain—and to run away through the thick green was his one way to survive. He had to get away. Sneak away. Death was behind him.

At the top of the mountain, our good doctor crashed through a curtain of trees and entered a topography of wild grass and bush. Before him was the open sky with its cold white stars, and, there in the distance, the ocean could be heard. He took three deep breaths, calmed himself a bit, saw a trail, and began to walk quickly down the mountain path to the coastline below.

From a helicopters perspective you could see that the aliens were road hogs and were driving above the speed limit. And that there to the right and below, slowly and serenely cruising up the curving road—on a collision course—the Johnson Family minivan. And you could see, from that cunning vantage point, an accident in the making. And some of you would have been terrified. And some of you would have been secretly thrilled. But none of you would have had long to wait. . . .

Mr. Johnson turned a corner and his field of vision ballooned with advancing alien horror. He hit the brakes, twisted the wheel, and slammed headlong into the mountainside. The van then rolled and rolled until it hit the stationary wheel of a bemused alien. (Superior unicycle bioengineering allowed the aliens to stop on a dime.)

The creature with the crumpled van at its "foot" turned to look back at its compatriots and gave what could have been a smile. It then leaned over the wreckage and began to gingerly peel off the roof. "Aw crap," thought the alien as it rummaged through the wreck, "They're all broken. . . . Wait, here's something. Oh, I don't think it's ripe enough." It pulled a two-year-old child still strapped to its safety seat from the wreck.

One of the alien's pals, read its mind and thought/said, "I'll try it." It took the offered infant and sucked the sips-worth of child-portion. The alien twisted its mouth and tossed the empty to the side of the road. "Ugh, yeaach—bitter!" it said in its way.

The aliens laughed and took to the road again.

Not so far below, he could make out the white raised relief of the ocean waves hitting the beach, and saw an orange glow, signifying the bonfire of the partying teens. He kept up his rapid pace down the coastal mountain trail, past manzanita bushes and fragrant bay trees. His mind was filled with apprehension and fear for the race of man. For Dr. Larry Seamons was no fool. He was familiar with the works of H.G. Wells and had seen the old movies too. He knew that these alien creatures were the masters of man, technically and intellectually. He knew that our military and scientists would not be able to stop them. That our only chance to defeat these conquering monsters lay in something small and unknown—in that something we take for granted and that is peculiar to our world and selves. That little special human thing was our salvation. Oh, how he hoped that was the case. Oh, how he hoped for a good science fiction ending to this science fiction nightmare hell!

His shoes touched the hard-packed sand and crunched down. And he looked down the beach at the bonfire and the swaying shadows that lined it. He would have to warn them! He moved his tired legs and made them run.

He was about fifty feet away from the kids when he started to yell, "Hey! Hey! Kids—Listen up! I've got to tell you something. You got to listen. Hey! There's monsters coming! Monsters!"

The drunk, stoned kids with layered hair and pastel-colored clothes danced to Van Halen's "Jump" and paid him no mind.

He ran forward, waving his arms, screaming, "Kids! Kids!"

One particularly good-looking preppy teen, wearing a blue and white pinstripe motif, turned and said, "Who is that asshole?"

Now all the teens checked out the weird guy running at them, and were working their wits for put-downs, when the aliens silently rolled up behind them.

The doctor's arms fell limp. His knees hit the sand. He covered his face with his hands and shook his head.

"Hey, what's wrong, Faggot?!" shouted an oblivious teen.

The doctor ignored the taunt—expecting the voice to be screaming in death agony at any moment. But the taunts still came. He looked up and saw that the monsters looked oddly uncomfortable and were edging away slowly from the beach.

"Hey you Faggot—You wanna come here? Faggot?"

"I'm gonna put my tape in now. OK, Danny? It's that new Huey Lewis everyone's listening to." The girl knelt to the boom box, hit a button, and fumbled in her bag for the important tape.

The music stopped. The aliens stopped. The monsters then began to roll forward . . . .

And the good doctor put two and two together and found the answer he was looking for. He got to his feet and ran toward the bonfire, shouting with a note of panic in his voice, "Kids! Kids! Don't stop the music! Don't stop the music!"

The Huey Lewis fan found her tape and popped it into the slot. She was just about to hit "play", when she looked behind and screamed. She was then pulled up and away.

Now all the teens joined the scream-your-heads-off chorus and began to get pulled up into the air.

And this time the good doctor ran towards the danger. He knew what to do. He dodged swinging alien arms and panicking teens and skidded like a baseball player stealing home—to reach the boom box. He made it. He got and grabbed that boom box with both hands . . . and then stared at it. Where was the "play" button? He felt a shadow and a chill at the back of his neck. "Oh god," he yelped as he began to smack the box with his hands and . . . and a radio station playing the hit singles of 1984 blasted out. And the hit song blasted the air clean and strong.

The aliens were stunned. It was as if they had smelled something terrible—so terrible that they could not comprehend it—and had to smell it again and again. Then one of the aliens retched.

The lead alien thought/said, "Oh, that's hideous. Oh! I've never heard anything . . . what is that?! Oh, let's get out of here. LETS GET OUT OF HERE!" It tossed all the teens it was holding away in disgust, spun on its wheel, and rolled hurriedly back up the mountainside. The two other aliens gratefully threw their kids and did the same. And Dr. Larry Seamons lay in the sand, and, although he hated the song, let it play on . . . .

The aliens returned to the ship with a case of humanoids. They had lucked-out and intercepted a Greyhound bus on the road home. And everything seemed fine enough, until later that night, as one of our earth-exploring aliens lay on its bunk and tried to sleep . . . . That tune! That horrible tune kept going through its head. It could not understand the lyrics—but it hated them, "What's love got to do, got to do with it? What's love but a second-hand emotion? What's love got to do, got to do with it? Who needs a heart when a heart can be broken?" And then this horrible little synthetic instrumental would start—and then the chant song would go on again . . . and again . . . and again. It just wouldn't leave its mind. The alien sweated, turned colors, and vomited over the side of its bunk.

It staggered to the ship's doctor, whom, upon entering the ailing creatures mind, yelped," Ugh, what is that? That? Phrasing? Ooh—what do you mean? That—oh no!" The insidious song now entered the doctor's mind. The captain rolled into the sickbay for a little chat and was instantly infected.

The aliens quickly left earth with the sick-making song stuck in their collective minds and headed for the nearest colony for medical help. And that colony within a week was infected and quarantined.

This type of musical mental affliction (what we call "earworms" or "musical hallucinations") was new to the aliens, and they had never built up the immunity. They had no concept of pop music, or even music, for that matter. Nearly two million aliens got sick, lost their minds and committed suicide due to the mind infection. Over three million had to be euthanized. A red dot was placed over planet Earth on all interstellar space maps. No one would ever visit it again for fear of going mad.

And there by the pool, meditating after doing her yoga exercises, sits Tina Turner. Her mind a calm, blank place—aware of only her own breathing and growing contentment—unaware of her singular role in saving the earth with her simple, catchy, shitty song. Don't you think we should thank her? How could we thank her? Perhaps, in tribute, we could just throw our heads back and sing her song to the stars. You know how it goes: "What's love got to do, got to do with it? What's love but a second hand emotion? What's love . . . ."

HAUNTED HOUSE-SITTING

Martha,

The number "4" has always held much importance in my life. Things seem to happen to me in fours . . . things that can only be described as "uncanny" or "macabre" or "coincidental." So it was with some trepidation that I noted the circled "4" of your note. The "4" read, "The apartment is haunted." I put the piece of paper down as my lips moved to form the silent words, "The apartment is haunted." And then again, "The apartment is haunted." And then again, "The apartment is haunted." I repeated that phrase, "The apartment is haunted," FOUR TIMES!!!(!) Out of the corner of my eye, I saw a flash of what only could be described as "ghostly white" slip into the bedroom. I ran in the opposite direction screaming like a seven-foot-tall football player IN FEAR!

Later, after gaining my composure, I decided to bring the ghost out. After all, I thought, it would be quite educational for me to talk with a dead person and find out the meanings and secrets of this life and afterlife. Ghosts must be as shy as miniature antelope, and as reclusive as pandas, I reasoned, otherwise we would see them more often. But they (ghosts) must feel more comfortable amongst their own kind! Perhaps, (I was thinking fast) these ghosts (or ghostie) would come out if they could be tricked into thinking that I was a ghost. If I could dress and look like a sneaky specter, perhaps said sneaky specter would show itself and maybe —just maybe—talk with me (or even dance!). I quickly ran into the bedroom and grabbed a sheet and threw it over my head! Then I sat down and waited!

After many hours I tired. No ghost had arrived and spoken to me. I pulled the sheet from my head and walked to the bathroom. I felt pretty disheartened, and it was with a sigh that I urinated. Then it struck me! If shy creatures such as ducks could be motivated to ponds to be shot at by hunters by DECOYS—why not ghosts?! I raced back to the bedroom carrying the black stand-up lamp (you know the one from the living room) and put it in the center of the room and draped a sheet over it—it didn't look right. I put my hat on it—now it was perfect! I then crawled under the bed and began my vigil. After many hours of concealment, I heard a voice that can only be described as "unworldly" say "Hi." My mind raced as fast as a race car going fast! The ghost was in the room and talking at the decoy—now what?!

Then a sense of "I know what to do" flooded over me like Caress Body Soap. I employed my talent of ventriloquism. I said in a voice thrown, "Hello. What is your name?"

The ghost said, "I am Nathan. Who are you?"

I said, "I am a ghost."

The ghost Nathan said, "No you're not," and disappeared.

I said, "No, No, I really am!" But the ghost had left, and no matter how much I pleaded to him to come back, he never returned.

James Bond vs. Santa

Chapter One: Arrival

The state-of-the-art, one-man helicopter streaked over the frozen ice mountains of Antarctica and clattered down to the floodlamp-ringed landing pad. As soon as the helicopter touched down, the landing pad began to lower with the high whine of hydraulic gears into the depths of the ancient tundra, the helicopter becoming smaller and smaller to the eye above, until it looked as if it were only an inch long, and one might imagine a child's arm snaking into frame to clumsily snatch the toy away.

As James Bond sat in his lowering helicopter, and as the ice-blue walls rose behind him, he removed his hood and parka and dark goggles. He straightened the tie of his tuxedo and checked his watch. He was prompt, and, although it had not been planned this way, he had been expected, or at least it began to appear that way. His assumptions proved correct: A dozen men in black with matching black knit caps and black machine guns waited for him as the lift cha-chunked to the ground floor. Bond exited the copter and with the single word, "Gentlemen . . ." was instantly taken into custody. The prudent Bond put aside his characteristic killing and mayhem and exploding firebombs and men being tossed over railings and thru windows until later . . . . First he would meet his prime target— and what better way than to be led to him with an armed escort?

A Plexiglas door whooshed open at a triggered sensor and Bond was ushered into a colossal supervillian-style complex. He was sat into a yellow golf cart. And with five golf carts before and five after him, the mini convoy began to snake its way with an electronic whine thru the seemingly unending corridors and open football-field-sized spaces of the secret compound. Bond noticed that many of the archways of the antiseptic, modern, militaristic superstructure had catch phrases like, "You Are a Helper," "Santa Needs You," "Claus Is Your Cause," and "Our Work Is Play" upon them. He also noticed, with the exception of a few sentries scattered about here and there, that the place was deserted.

The cavalcade of carts entered a huge, high-ceilinged lobby and stopped at a gigantic green door. And Bond was shoved out and left alone. . . .

Chapter Two: Behind The Green Door

The titanic green door opened easily upon its well-balanced hinges and Bond entered the most fantastic Christmas office party he had ever seen! The room was larger than a flayed blimp, was filled with scores of long tables laden with sparkling china and glass, had a window-wall with a holographic view of a rolling ocean, had a jazz combo with Lalo Schifrin on piano playing Latin jazz on a rotating circular stage, and was filled with living butterflies that bounced over tables to light upon delighted noses. And the Christmas party was for the hundreds of elves that worked within the secret underground superstructure of the super villain that British Intelligence said was planning on destroying the free world—a super villain known as Santa!

Bond was somewhat relieved to see that the elves did not resemble the small, childishly composed creatures of TV's "Rudolph the Red-Nosed Reindeer," but were rather more like the humanized, effete, and noble types of "The Lord of the Rings" trilogy by Australian filmmaker, Peter Jackson.

The elves seemed to be having a good time: laughing and eating, flirting and drinking. An elfin waiter quick-stepped up to Bond, and with a "This way sir," gave him a corner seat at the end of a long table. Again, Bond was pleased that he had the forbearance of mind to wear his tuxedo. The elves were exquisitely dressed in the finest fashions of Los Angeles. Bond was given a choice of either "Steak" or "Salmon" or a "Vegetarian Lasagna." Bond chose the steak "Rare: Let it bleed." He then grabbed a bottle of wine from the table, poured himself a glass and topped-off the glass next to his. A female voice said, "Thank you, Mr. Bond," and he turned into the face of the most beautiful elf on the planet!

Bond was a man, perhaps even more than a man compared to most, and his penis filled with hot blood to three-quarters full at the sight of the elfin babe. She had Elizabeth Taylor eyes, a Nicole Kidman nose, the eyebrows of Anne Hathaway and the large, full lips of Don Knotts—but in a sensuous and feminine way. Although she was seated, he surmised her to be tall and not willowy in figure, but pound for pound perfectly turned in shape and design, as if she had been drawn by the hand of a Disney animator in a heated, semen-fever dream. Her ears were slightly large and pointed.

James Bond took his wine glass and held it before the elf. "You have me at a disadvantage," he said.

The elf showed her pretty teeth and said, "My name's Myrathdral Turaucch-Teratina."

"I'll call you Tina," charmed Bond as they clinked glasses in toast.

While he ate his steak, the master spy learned that the elves had been working for Santa for just under a year, that they had produced millions upon millions of toys and clothing and electronic goods ("Elfin Technology is superior to Sony")—that Tina worked in Marketing—her specialty being in consumer research—and that the elves worshipped Santa as their god, and had worked for Santa centuries ago but were called back just this year and were only too happy to fulfill his wishes again. . . .

Bond felt a hand squeeze his thigh and heard, "You are a sexy man." He saw the elf's eyes shine with third-glass-of-wine-lust. "I'd like to meet this Santa of yours," said Bond.

"You will . . . he wants to meet you too . . . but not now."

The elf's hand remained on his leg.

Bond looked at her close-up face and like a German expressionist movie of the 30s the hand-scripted words, "Pump her for information" appeared across her forehead.

A senior elf took the circular stage and introduced the company Christmas party raffle.

"Let's get out of here," breathed the electric elf, "I never win."

Bond stroked and squeezed her thigh, "Never say never," he leered. . . .

Chapter Three: Bond's Elf Lesson

The nude elf knelt on the carpet before the naked, wide-spread legs of Bond. . . .

Bond lowered himself to a kneeling position, exposing his muscular and surprisingly large ass. He moved forward to kiss her, but she stopped him. . . . Bond was to become an initiate in Elfin Sex. . . . She leaned forward until her mouth was about a half an inch away from his. Opening her mouth wide, she began to breathe rapidly with a "Huh-huh-huh-huh" chant-grunt. Bond mimicked her—and their breath entered each others' mouths and the rhythm and the sounds and the closeness began to fill Bond with a "Huh-huh-huh" passion-fuck-lust. The "Huh-huh-huh-huh-huh-huh" continued until the elf saw that Bond was no longer Bond, but a red blaze of tension turned to tension turned to tension and she threw herself back and Bond sprang. Mouths met. Tongues pressed and slipped. Hands grabbed hold and pulled and pulled and pushed and slipped in and out. A head and hair flopped over a groin and an elfin tongue flicked over a British cockhead like a hummingbird's wing. And a man cried, "Ughhhrrr—No!" as he pulled the head away to throw himself into elfish hot wet delight. And then the humping, pumping, pushing, slamming, shoving. An earlobe tongue-tipped. A nipple lipped and teeth-tipped. A leg thrust. A head thrown. A neck flushed and face flushed and a grimace and a groan—a cry-moan and shriek!

Afterwards, Bond would describe Elfin Sex as "magical, enchanting, but in a very nasty, nasty way."

Chapter Four: Bond's Elf Lesson Part Two

Bond lay sprawled upon the carpet as the nude elf leaned forward to light a cigarette. She passed it and settled back into his arms. Bond took a drag and as a gag said, "Don't elves smoke after sex?"

She said, "I've never checked." She then stood and arched backwards, exposing her enflamed and cum-smeared vagina for him to inspect.

As Bond laughed, a thin green smoke erupted from her elfin vagina into his face. He fell forward—faster than one might think possible—to hit the carpet face down—unconscious!

The Elfin temptress walked over to a wall and pressed a button with the air of a business woman who had majored in Marketing.

Chapter Five: A Gift For Santa

Bond came-to in a barren, concrete room, tied to a chair and fully clothed: An elfish sense of modesty prompted his now being dressed, he correctly assumed. He shook his head and tried to clear his mind of the drug. He would never look at a vagina with the same innocence.

Bond managed to press a button on his watch and a small blade flicked out and he began to work on the rope when Santa appeared. The Santa just popped into the room like some cheap trick of editing as on "I Dream of Jeannie." Bond was taken aback—first by the entrance—second by the size of the man. Santa was a giant of a man, over seven feet tall, and built like a wrestler, with a veined and muscle-bound neck that should have had a gangland tattoo on it. Santa's suit was what to be expected. His white beard, however, was closely cropped, as was his moustache.

Santa stared into Bond's eyes, shook his head, took off his gloves and cracked his knuckles.

"Do you expect me to talk?" said Bond.

"No," said Santa, "I expect you to listen."

Santa squatted on his haunches before Bond, saying, "You don't understand me. All I want to do is give the good boys and girls a gift this year. I've decided that this is the time to bring back the tradition . . . and expand upon it to include good adults too. That's all, to give gifts . . . whatever could be wrong by that?"

The hands of Bond diligently worked the ropes while the mouth of Bond said, "Sure, sounds simple, just flood the market with free gifts, thereby destroying the economy of the western world—a business world that depends on Christmas to keep afloat. Sure, sounds simple enough. I don't see how you can do it though."

"My dear Mr. Bond, don't you believe in Santa?"

Bond smiled and said, "I believe in economic terrorism."

Bond then listened as Santa explained that his intentions were purely altruistic; that he had done it before and would do it again; that he was centuries old and was, in fact, a god; that he could travel at the speed of light; and that, again, the economy might be bruised but not broken because not everyone would get a gift—only the good!

"And you of course are the moral arbitrator of good and evil. Just what is your criteria, if I may ask?" said Bond as he worked loose the final strand of his bond.

The elfin god responded warmly, "Only kindness. Only by the acts of kindness that men give. You can be a kind man, Bond, I know. The world will become a kinder place to live in after a few years of my rewards."

As the knife cut the final strand, Bond stamped his foot and a switchblade jutted out from the tip of his shoe. He said, "'Tis the Season of Sharing . . . Take this!" And he kicked the knife-shoe at the belly of Santa!

Chapter Six: A Quick Fight

Now everything freezes and we revolve to see a side view of the action:

Bond with a smiling grimace, eyes bulging in the effort of the kick; Santa leaning back with unnatural flexibility; the extended leg and the blade of Bond pointing above the Santa body. We revolve behind Santa and now the action moves in slow-motion: the kick-blade swings over Santa; Santa back-flips . . . and then turns to his attacker with arms and legs assuming the Kung Fu position "Crane."

Bond flies at Santa's throat. Santa grabs Bond by his throat and lifts the amazed and struggling Bond into the air—holding him three feet off the ground. Bond slams his fists onto Santa's ears. Santa screams and Bond falls to the floor. Santa steps on Bond's neck and presses down hard. Bond grabs the foot, the ankle, tries to wriggle free, but is trapped. Bond begins to turn red. Santa presses down unrelenting. Bond begins to sputter and gasp. Santa grins. And then Bond, in a very athletic maneuver, flips his body up and kicks his foot-shoe-blade deep into Santa's chest. Santa looks confused, spurts blood from his mouth, and then, like a Christmas tree falling, crashes to the floor. Bond checks the old elf's pulse. Santa is dead.

Chapter Seven: Santa?

Bond wiped the blood off his blade and reinserted it into his shoe, and was about to toss the sopping handkerchief aside, when the door whooshed open and Elf Tina walked in. She became a hysterical parakeet: shrieking, bouncing off walls, flapping her arms and losing feathers—from her holiday boa. She finally landed by the side of the fallen Santa and wept up into the face of Bond the question, "Why?"

Bond grimly replied, "It had to be done."

Tina flew into a ridiculing tirade that accurately assessed the reasons for Bond's killing actions. Bond wildly flailed at every accurate smash serve of logic Tina volleyed at him, like a man trying to play tennis with a ping-pong paddle. It was all true: He had killed a man just to keep a corrupt and failing way of life a bit more secure in its status quo; he was a killer without a heart or conscious; he may have killed a good and righteous god; he had accomplished nothing but pain and woe and. . . .

Bond tossed the bloody handkerchief aside and said, "Got to go," and briskly walked past the elfin beauty.

"Wait," said Tina, "it'll be quicker if I escort you. And I don't want you killing any more innocent elves."

Chapter Eight: Secret Santa

The giant Santa lay in the vacant room like a dead elephant seal in an empty swimming pool. Then with a champagne cork "Pop!" the Santa body disappeared—and with a dramatic "Bang!" and flash of smoke—a new Santa appeared! The Santa quickly began to laugh a deep and hearty, "Ho-Ho-Ho-Ho-Ho." It stopped and placed its forefinger to the side of its nose. And then the finger moved to pick the nose. And then Santa disappeared altogether, leaving the vacant room very empty—as empty as a Christmas stocking on December 26th. . . .

Chapter Nine: Bond's Christmas Surprise

James Bond nestled into his silken sheets, sleeping deeply in his bed in London. Across the large, luxury studio apartment, the curtains heaved in and out as if in response to a giant's breath. A small, sparkling Christmas tree sat upon a work desk, a testament to Bond's attempt to normalize and conform. Bond rolled over and happily engaged in his favorite dream of "The Scuba Girls and The Big Fight and The Happy Ending," as a large figure blinked into the center of the room. The figure stood in the shadows of the darkened room and used its almost omnipresent powers to deduce if Bond was truly asleep. Satisfied, the not-so-mysterious figure of Santa whizzed in a streak of red and white to Bond's computer—hacked into it—and changed all information Intelligence had gathered on the location of the secret compound in Antarctica. The next instant found Santa standing before the rather pathetic artificial Christmas tree. His gloved hands put a gaily wrapped present under the tree. A note upon the present read, " To My Favorite Spy From Santa P.S. Be Kind."

Bond awoke that Christmas morn later than normal. He put his bare feet to the floor, walked to the bathroom, then put on the coffee, took a shower, drank his coffee, read a little Conan Doyle, and then walked back to the bathroom—used it—and then on the way back to his book, noticed the present under the tree. He read the note and, without lifting the box, bent to sniff the package. (His trained nose could smell explosives!) He smelled nothing dangerous. He smiled and relaxed his body and picked up the gift—toying with it by tossing it into the air and catching it. He moved to the couch and threw himself down into it. He tore off the wrapping and with a gleam in his eye opened the box. And then Bond did a rare thing . . . he giggled with glee.

Bond pulled a classic 1952 Beretta Automatic out of the box and checked it for heft and then cleanliness, although he could already tell that it had never been used. He then noticed, peeking through the tissue paper, a light, chamois, leather holster, and snatched it up. With a real shout-laugh, Bond stood and put on the holster and put the gun into its nest. He then ran to the mirror and practiced looking poker-faced and then pulling the gun. Bond was quick—very quick—with his new toy.

But playtime ended swiftly for Bond (as it always did) as his suspicious mind moved him to the computer. Yes, information had been erased and changed. His report on eliminating "Red Menace" was still there, but again, the information on the underground compound was different than he remembered it to be. . . .

Bond went back to the couch and sat and here are some of his thoughts: "Guess I didn't kill him. The body was dead. A stand-in? Don't think so, doesn't fit the profile. They'll probably send me out again—finish the job right. Think I can remember where that mad house was. Location information tampered with and useless now—think I can remember where. . . . So, they'll send me out again . . . or will they? So people got gifts? No threat to national security there. Some companies get upset . . . so what? Maybe "M" got a gift and is thinking the same thing I am now. No, she's not going to get any gift from Santa—not that bitch. Even if they do send me back, I don't think I could take him: moves faster than light, is a god . . . is a bloody god of the elves. Christ! I'll turn the job down. Screw em!

Some crazy Santa Claus wants to make the world a better place by doing his crazy thing—so what?! Oh, who knows, maybe they'll just drop the whole thing—that's what I want to do. "Be kind," he says. Guess I could just drop the whole thing myself. Not report that I got the gift—and not report the tampered computer info. And not be a good boy or be a good boy or uh. . . ."

Bond heaved a great sigh and pulled the new gun from its holster. He looked at it and just couldn't help but smile at it. "What the hell," he said aloud, "I ain't doing a thing."

In a world of gods and elves and men, Bond was just a spy, and damn it—he liked his new toy!

Easy Going

Billy Rainer never did much planning. He wasn't a good scout. He took what came his way and made the best of it. He had lived all of his sixty-four years in the town of Fresno, making the best of it. A bus or a train or a plane to someplace else had never come his way, and he liked the smells and sights and comforts of the place he was in. "Move away where? I got what I need here," he had said to the fertilizer salesman, whom he faced across the scratched linoleum table, as he picked up his three cards.

"Yeah, I'm sure you do," said the salesman with a patronizing smirk, as he dealt himself two.

The afternoon bar was quiet and dark: a box in the middle of a very hot empty street; Billy and the salesman playing cards; the bartender smoking and drinking beer from a glass and watching a pitching duel on the small color TV.

The salesman called the bet and lost four nickels. A mild anger rose low in his chest, but he pushed it down. He wouldn't leave until he had won. Billy took the deck and shuffled with a cig planted in his smile. As he tossed out the hand, the bar door creaked open and slammed shut, allowing a figure to enter in a flash of smoky sunlight. It was a young woman of twenty-two.

The woman said into the bar, "Hey Billy, ready to go?"

Billy pulled the cigarette from his mouth to grin with all his teeth at the girl. "In a minute, Becky."

The bartender asked the young woman if she wanted a drink, and when it was declined, where she and Billy were off to. She said they were going to the Bell Market to get some groceries for tonight's dinner. The bartender said that there was a sale on chuck roast at the Bell Market and gave the young woman a simple recipe for it that contained only salt, pepper, a can of tomato sauce and a packet of Lipton Onion Soup Mix. The young woman listened with eager interest, and as she said, "We'll try it tonight," Billy pushed back his chair, rose and said, "That was real fun. I'm sorry to leave with all your money—but I can't keep my Becky waitin."

"Sixty-five cents ain't all my money," said the salesman sharply, but then cooled himself down fast. He was new in town and he didn't want to make any enemies—so he added genially, "Ok, Mr. Lucky, go ahead and have fun with your daughter. I'll get my money back the next time, eh?"

Billy smiled and gave the salesman a friendly and gentle pat on the shoulder. He then walked up to the young woman and put his arm around her shoulder. Together, they opened the door, left the bar, and walked into the sun.

As the bartender and the salesman poured beer into their glasses, the bartender told the salesman that Becky wasn't Billy's daughter but his girlfriend. The salesman was astonished at the queerness of it—old man . . . young girl? "What? A good-looking girl like that?! What possibly could a good-looking girl like that see in an old fart?!"

"Well, you got me there," said the bartender. But after taking a sip, he added, "But that Billy does have his qualities. Everybody in town likes him."

As Billy drove down the boulevard and felt the hot wind hit his arm and face, he thought about being called, "Mr. Lucky." He looked over at Becky and then back at the road. "I guess I am lucky, I guess," he thought. He then smiled again—his face was used to smiling. "I guess I'm lucky to be alive and in Fresno again," he said to himself.

Space Pants

When I arrived on this planet more than two hundred years ago, I was inquisitive and resourceful. My mission was to observe human behavior without being detected. If humanity proved itself worthy of domestication, future contact would be made. If however the standard criteria were not met, standard disposal would naturally result.

Being young and resourceful, I used the ALCOM to design my body into an article of human clothing. What better way to intimately observe my subject," thought I, "than to be worn on the said subject's person?" I would become a silent symbiotic partner, providing my host protection from the elements with comfort and style, whilst satisfying my own hunger for knowledge. If I wished to study differing social structures and variables unknown, I could change the look of my disguise in accordance with the human concepts of fashion. . . . That is how I came to be a pair of pants. And that is how I have come to know the lives of coal miners and kings and window washers and secretaries and shark hunters and rednecks and poets and rap stars and grape pickers and mommies and daddies and aging queens and Martha and the Vandellas and presidents and streetwalkers.

I have learned a lot about this human race, and sadly, I am not impressed . . . They cannot be domesticated. They do not take crowding or solitary captivity well. And they are not cute or affectionate either. These dull creatures will destroy themselves far earlier than my original anticipations, and I will not be picked up in time. There is also a great chance I will be destroyed along with them. Oh yes, I have learned over the years to hate my hosts (and their so-called cultures) and look forward in a way to the time when they do blow their moronic heads off. These sorry creatures, these humans, have one big plus however: They certainly are juicy and delicious.

As I mentioned earlier, when I first arrived I was inquisitive and resourceful. Today I am no longer inquisitive, but still if I may say so, I continue to be rather resourceful. This morning I caught a nice fat one. As he approached me in the rack of the used clothing store, I noted his appearance and style and quickly tailored myself into a beautiful pair of black pleated cotton twill pants with hideaway zipper and button-down back pockets. I had this guy hooked. He could wear me everywhere: to the office, on dates, at home in front of the TV—everywhere. I mean, I was more versatile than a pair of black jeans. When he put me on, I became so soft and comfortable the slob actually mooed. I had him.

He wore me proudly out of that store and into a bar. Then he started drinking and talking, crowding the smokey air with opinions. I tried not to listen. A long time ago I did a longitudinal study and learned that human values and opinions shift with the passage of time and events. What one man holds dear today may be hostilely denied tomorrow. Most human opinions are not well-formed enough to withstand the bludgeoning of real events and are consequently discarded or modified—modified of course into new, fanciful projections of ego desire. Yes, I gave up listening to humans a long time ago. I decided to savor my carnal environment instead. . . .

Ahh, the heated body, soft and pliant. The flavor of the sweet salt of sweat, the acrid, moist musk of soiled underpants. Mmmm, I was gently grazing on a succulent blackhead when my host gave up his bar stool and left for home.

My host's apartment was what I expected, a lonely jumble of tasteless furniture and frayed poster art. All the articles and apparel of a clumsy trip through a life were there. I let him void his bowels before springing into action.

First I changed the fabric of my body into Xorbital 5, an extremely dense plastic. Then I slammed down to one-third my original size. Naturally his hips and legs were instantly pulverized. You know of course that with every action there is an equal and opposite reaction, so with the massive upward rush of pressure, his heart exploded, his mouth blasted blood, his eyeballs splattered the TV screen, and his eardrums became bloody yo-yos.

I relaxed my hold, allowing the spicy juices to seep back into the open wounds. I didn't want to waste a drop. I dined on a soup of blood and adipose tissue, absorbing all the soft, sweet stuff I could. To be frank, I wasn't all that hungry, but I ate as much as I could. Once you have gotten used to eating a lot, you do it as much as you can, I guess. Anyway I sucked that fat cherry dry.

Now it was time to vacate the premises. I can't move very far or fast, but by contracting and expanding my body, I inched my way off my host and into a nearby corner. I then changed myself into a pair of women's Capri pants: black, unobtrusive, functional. And with my body satiated, gorged even, I fell into a little slumber, the buzzing of happy flies providing my lullaby.

Now I wait. In time the body will be discovered, relatives or the city will move in and clean the joint up, and I will either be given away or sold to a used clothing store. The hunt begins again.

Being marooned on this sinking tub of a planet is a lonely business. Although life is accelerated here, time seems to move so, so very slowly. Without the sharing of thoughts, my thoughts themselves have become personal game pieces. I end up playing thinking games devoid of meaning. I have become lonely and embittered, and I'm afraid, mad. My only solace in this life is my gluttony.

So I wait. Perhaps I'll devour a waitress or a policeman. Perhaps I'll devour a mayor or a delivery boy. Perhaps I'll devour you, whoever you may be. For remember you all are equal in my eye. You all put your pants on . . . one leg at a time.

Practical Tales for Children

Tommy the Nail

Bill and Mary Toothbrush

Tofu

Charles the Paperclip

Indian Bowl

Tommy The Nail

Once upon a time, there lived a nail named Tommy. He lived a happy life with his friends in a box.

One day, Tommy's friend told him about the big black hammer named Lionel, how that Lionel would smash bad little nails on the head and bend them up and sometimes break them in two. Tommy said that he wasn't afraid of Lionel. His daddy told him that hammers were a rough lot, but that the nail and the hammer worked hand in hand and made things work right in this world.

The next day, Tommy saw Lionel real close. The hammer looked like a giant to little Tommy. Tommy tried to say, "Hi," but the hammer just banged him on the head.

BAM. BAM. BAM.

Tommy was in a coma for months. When he came to, he could not move or see. He felt cool air touch the top of his head. He started to cry. He cried for a long time, until Lionel the Hammer, came up to him. Lionel told Tommy the Nail to be quiet. Tommy told Lionel the Hammer that he was scared and didn't like the horrible, trapped feeling he had, and that he missed being able to move and see.

Lionel the Hammer told him, "It's for the community good."

The End

BILL AND MARY TOOTHBRUSH

Bill the Toothbrush hung in his holder, face-to-face with his love, Mary the Toothbrush. He would spend all day staring at Mary, feeling great love, until he was put under the faucet and creamed and then jammed into someone's mouth. But he was a toothbrush, he didn't mind the work, and he was in love.

One day Mary said, " I don't love you anymore."

Bill asked, "Why?"

Mary said, "I don't know, really. I just can't stand the sight of your face anymore."

Bill sobbed, "I'm sorry."

Mary said, "I hate your sorry face."

Bill said, "But, I still love you."

Mary said, "That's life."

Bill asked, "What are we to do?"

Mary said, " I don't know."

The two hung around each other for longer than you would expect, until one was thrown away and replaced.

The End

Tofu

Once upon a time, there lived a chunk of Tofu that had a strange way of thinking. The Tofu had seen much of life and had suffered much. Whatever the Tofu wanted in this world—had been declined. Whatever the world offered—the Tofu declined. You see, there was a disparity between desire and opportunity. And this led to unhappiness. Therefore, the Tofu developed a philosophy to make life bearable.

When asked about its strange philosophy, the Tofu would say, "All sadness comes from desire. Eliminate desire (or hope) and welcome peace. Happiness is the illusion of desire fulfilled. There is no such thing as the illusion 'happiness.' If there is no happiness, there is no unhappiness. If I cease to desire the illusory, my desire becomes commonplace and dies. Without desire, life is lived moment by moment in the wonderful NOW. . . ."

"I live my life in a rational peace."

The Tofu lived a quiet, well-balanced life. Some found the Tofu to be a little bland.

The End

CHARLES THE PAPERCLIP

Once upon a time, there was a paperclip named Charles, and he held things together. The collection of papers he secured were thankful for Charles, for he made them a unit of cohesive importance. Together, and only together, the papers knew their lives would have meaning. Together, they made a document and documents were important things and depended upon order. Charles held the pages in order. He was strong. He was firm. And he was proud.

One day Charles and his group were picked up and thrown into a box filled with others like themselves—documents.

"Hi-Hi!" shouted a binder clip, "Who wants to join us?"

"I am Charles!" said the paperclip, "I have many pages. I hold things together."

"My name's Ted. Below me is Tom and Terrance and Franklin and Ray—we're all clips to paper—and we all hold things together."

"We hold things together!" yelled Tom, Terrance, Franklin, and Ray.

"We hold things together!" yelled Ted.

The papers began to shut out their numbers in turn.

"We hold things together!" shouted Charles, joining the chorus, as the clips and their numbered pages were loaded into a truck and driven to the dump.

The End

Indian Bowl

The Chief was an American Indian bowl the size of a cantaloupe. He was woven out of reeds and had bright picture designs on his side. He sat on a mantel with Udo (the German Stein), Piet (the Dutch Vase), and John Wayne (the Commemorative Plate). The stein, vase, and plate were his good friends, and they enjoyed each other's company. The Chief's friends revered him, for he was said to be a ceremonial bowl from a tribe of Indians that had all died long ago. Every night, John Wayne and the Chief would tell stories of the old fights between the cowboys and Indians. John Wayne would have the cowboys win. And the Chief would have the Indians win—through cunning. Piet and Udo loved to hear the stories; it didn't matter to them who won. The tales that the bowl and the plate told were make-believe. They had never been in any wars. The fun was in the telling.

From their place on the mantel, the bowl and the plate and the vase and the stein looked down upon the other objects that served in the living room. . . .

A new friend! A beautiful, porcelain figurine of a little girl holding a bucket came to stay on the mantel. She was made in Hong Kong and spoke with an accent. The Chief was in love. He told her all about himself and his great deeds as a ceremonial bowl. And she smiled with interest. She said she was an imitation of a famous Dresden figurine. The Chief had never heard of this word "imitation." She said that the word meant a "reproduction" or "copy" of an original something. The Chief thought about this. . . . He remembered being made by young Indian hands. He remembered the young Indian being proud of him. He remembered being taken to the store where the shopkeeper thought he was wonderful. He remembered how he was bought for a lot of money by his masters because he was so wonderful. "I am an original," he said. His new friend was happy to agree.

One special, crazy day, the Chief was taken off the mantel and dusted and placed gingerly into a box filled with tissue paper. He then was moved about for some time, until his masters took him from the box and handed him to someone else. This someone else was an appraiser, an expert who judged the true value of rare objects. He was handled gently and questions about his place of birth and age were asked. His masters answered the questions and said how much they had paid for him. They were told that they had paid far too much money and words like "modern" and "common" were used. The Chief was an Indian bowl, made by an Indian—but he was not an ancient ceremonial bowl made long ago. He was made to be sold to tourists and had little value. His masters tossed him back into his box in a rough way.

The Chief never saw his friends on the mantel again. He was taken to the garage, to the master's workshop. He was put on a rough wooden shelf and filled with old rusty sharp things. There were lots of spiders in the dark garage.

"When I was young," thought the Chief to himself, "I was told that I was uncommon and beautiful and I believed these things. And I grew up proud. Now I am told that I am just a normal, nothing bowl, that I am not special, that I am just like anything else. This is hard to take, and I don't know if I can. . . ."

"But one thing I do know," said the Chief resolutely to himself. "If I am to work for the master, and if my role, or place, is to hold things, then I will do my best. My pride may have been misguided, but I still have my pride for all it's worth, and I will do my job well."

The Chief stayed in the workshop and held nails. He made new friends and told tales of cowboys and Indians. He thought about his days on the mantel and his lost friends less and less. He accepted his new position in the world with quiet resignation. He never got used to the feeling of the nails inside him.

The End

Making Friends

This is the story of all the strange things that have happened to me, and how I saved the planet. . . .

It all started about six months ago when I was coming home from my job as an assistant processing clerk for Green Cine, and it was late at night—around 3:00 in the morning—and no one was on the road. I was driving up to the narrow bridge that crosses Butler Creek when I saw them. There were four of them standing in the road blocking the bridge. They were alien monster men—about seven feet tall with thick green skin and weird angular heads—and I stopped the car. I knew I was in deep shit. As the monsters approached me I felt like a kid in grammar school who had done something wrong (when it wasn't my fault!) and was being sent to the principal's office. I felt powerless and scared and angry. The aliens took me from my car and somehow put me to sleep. I still have dreamlike memories of being hit with a beam of light that made my insides feel like they were filled with soda water, and I remember doing a lot of screaming. Then the next thing I knew, I was back in my car, all alone and feeling real tired. I drove the short distance home and like a robot took off my clothes and went to bed.

The next day when I woke up, I was all feverish and sweaty. I got out of bed to have a drink of water from the bathroom sink. I grabbed the glass and filled it, and was drinking the water when I saw myself in the mirror. I was sweating blood. I yelled, dropped the glass, and loped to the phone. My heart was pounding and I was panicky. When I opened the door for the paramedics, they freaked out and I fainted.

I was at the local hospital for about a week, and I could tell that they didn't know what to do about me there. My bleeding stopped on its own, but I still had a high fever and something was happening to my insides that the doctors were baffled by. I told them about my alien abduction story, but because of my fever, I think they thought

I was babbling nonsense. Finally, I think someone must have taken me seriously because this big government hotshot doctor named Dr. Feifer came to see me. He wanted to hear my story and I told him the whole thing. He believed me and that made me feel better. I asked him what was happening to me and if he could cure me. He said that he didn't know but that he wanted to help. The next day, I was put into a helicopter and taken to some government hospital somewhere. It was a long trip and no one talked to me the whole time.

At the hospital place, I was put into this big room and everyone treated me like I was radioactive or something. They all wore big space suits and wouldn't touch me directly—if you've seen "The Andromeda Strain," or even "Independence Day," you know the scene. All that the doctors would do was test me—take blood and x-ray me—and my condition just got worse. It felt like I had gas pains all over my body, and I could feel my innards shifting and squirreling into new positions. And I knew what was happening to me. I was becoming a monster. I was changing into an alien monster. I was like the Wolfman who turns from man into monster. But unlike the horror film hack who changes from homely sad sack into hairy-scary in quick time-lapse photography, my change was slow—like watching a plant grow—and it hurt like hell.

But you know the worst part of this whole thing was that I felt so alone. No one talked to me. No one treated me like I was a real person, only a thing to be looked at and touched with a ten-foot pole. Dr. Feifer would see me everyday, and he seemed nervous and looked at my face with quick sidelong glances and wouldn't answer me when I asked him questions. I have friends and a brother and a mother and I wanted to talk to them—but he wouldn't let me—he wouldn't let anyone talk to me—and I wanted to talk so bad. It made me crazy not being able to say anything to anybody and then have them say things back. I started talking to myself and that helped a bit, but not enough.

I had never felt so very, very lonely—so apart and separate from everything—and I admit that I prayed to have someone to share things with. I prayed for a friend.

A few months later my prayers were answered. I saw him looking at me through the observation window. He smiled at me and waved. I raised my arm to wave back and snapped through the restraining strap to do so. He walked into the room (without using the door) and came right up to me. He was happy to see me and I was happy to see him. It was like meeting your best friend that you hadn't seen since you were a kid and nothing had changed, except that you were older—but then all of a sudden there you were—best friends again! Of course, I don't think I had ever met this guy before. He was an alien monster man. But then again now so was I. But it felt like I had known him all my life.

He said, "How are you doing?" You feel all right?"

I said, " Yeah, yeah, I sure do."

He said, "Let's get out of here."

And we walked through walls, past screaming men shooting guns, to the spaceship parked outside and then left the planet.

The ship was full of friendly faces and I was real excited—asking questions and joking around. They thought I was pretty witty and these guys had a sense of humor too. One of the things I wanted to know was why? Why had they made me into one of them? They said they did it for reasons of communication; once literally inside their shoes, so to speak, you could understand their point of view and they understood you better also. It's true that I instantly knew their language and how their minds ticked. These people were very compassionate and logical and hated waste. They truly loved one another and loved me also. I had never felt this loved before, except maybe by my parents and brother when I was real little.

I was taken to this room and put before the ruling elders of the ship. You see, these guys wanted my input on the future of our planet. They explained their mission to me. Besides colonization, it was their job to collect planets that were used up and then make new planets from the old material. They recycled planets. The elders thought that our planet was just about all used up—that in a few years we would kill ourselves and everything else on Earth. One thing they could do was to recycle it now, while they were in the area, instead of waiting for it to be unpopulated. They could just destroy all life and get the materials now. It would be like when you or I would recycle a bottle of beer. There is always a little left over in the bottle—you just shake it out into the sink and then throw it into the bin—except humanity was the left over beer. This idea frightened me. I said, "Are you sure we're going to destroy ourselves and the planet?"

They said that because of our propensity for war and lack of respect for the environment we were sure to die.

I told them that many people fought against war and wanted to preserve the environment. That we knew those things were big problems. But we were working on it.

The elders just stared at me sadly.

I thought fast and hard. "Wait," I said. "What if you didn't kill everyone? What if you just killed the Republicans?"

The elders leaned forward in interest.

I hurried on, " You see they're the ones who just live for the moment and are greedy and don't care about anyone else or the environment or the wars and they stand in the way of doing the right things and if we uh, uh. . . ." I stopped. I knew what I was saying was wrong. They were just people—those Republicans—and there's something about people that makes them think about themselves too much, and not about the other guy enough, and go for the quick answer and then make mistakes. I sighed. I looked down and said, "No that's wrong. That won't work. I don't think killing anyone is the answer."

The elders nodded and smiled at me, and I felt flooded by the warmth of their love. I was a little overcome and I stammered, " I just wish everyone could feel like me right now . . . I, oh. . . ." I trailed off and then I began to cry.

One of the elders reached over and took my hand. He gave it a squeeze and said, " We are compatible—you and I."

The elders closed their eyes and nodded again. They knew what to do.

After that, everyone on the planet got hit with a bright light and felt their insides filled with soda water and sweated blood and got gas pains all over and became like me. And now when I meet Dr. Feifer we look at each other straight in the eye and we talk easily as friends. For we are all friends now—we're Traktorians—what else could we be but friends! Traktorians love and respect Traktorians! Yes, this world is a much nicer and easygoing place to be in now that we all work together as friends. I think the planet likes us too . . . now that we've changed for the better.

THE LAST WISH

Once upon a time, there lived an unusual man. This man, let's say his name was Perry, had never touched himself in a sexual way. He was thirty-seven years old and had never masturbated. Perry had never experienced sex with a woman either. He was a virgin.

Finally, on one beautiful spring morning, Perry could not stand the pressures of his groin any longer and tore off his pants and underwear. Spitting out his first sacrilegious oath as he grabbed his burgeoning boner, he averted his eyes from the cross on the wall and began to form certain images in his mind. . . .

His hands smoked friction against his pleasure pole. His eyes pressed shut-tight. His mind became a pornographer's palate of perversion—a veritable parade of pimp and prostitute. And the palm penile pressure increased. His lips quivered. His legs bucked. His masturbating hand became a blur . . . . He arched his back and squealed in orgasm. From the tip of his penis a stream of smoke shot across the room and a genie appeared. The astonished Perry lay on his back, on his bed, with his dick in his hand as the genie said, " You have three wishes. Be careful of what you wish, for it will come true."

Perry's mind was quick and adaptive. He did not question the existence of the genie and understood his words . . . and, being an unusual man, did not ask the genie for money, or women, or the power of invisibility or flight. He sat up straight and said, "I would like to be able to make things grow . . . you know, plants and things. I would like to help life along."

The genie nodded, said the traditional "Your wish is my command," and clapped his hands. Perry felt a strange whisping shiver, as if his ass were being tickled with a feather. The genie smiled and said, "It has been done. I shall now return to my prison until you require me again."

With a flash of smoke the genie vanished and snaked his way back into the narrow opening of Perry's meatus.

Perry was very excited. He quickly dressed and left home. He could hardly wait to put his newfound talent to task.

Singlehandedly, Perry grew great gardens, brought life to the world's deserts, saved the rainforests, ended starvation, stopped the greenhouse effect and gave cancer to every human being he touched. It seemed that Perry's touch caused unbounded cellular growth.

Perry, although loved and revered by humanity, was banished to a deserted island. He lived alone in a mansion surrounded by a jungle, with no one to talk to but monkeys and birds.

One spring night, as he lay listening to the cries of the jungle, he pulled his penis from his pajamas and began to stroke. . . . Four minutes later, with a puff of smoke, the genie appeared.

"Your wish is my command," said the genie.

"I would like to talk to the animals . . . to communicate fully with all the beasts of heaven and earth."

The genie waved his hand, and Perry felt the same strange tickling sensation. The genie said, " You have but one wish left . . . . When you want me . . . you know where to find me."

With a puff and a flash the genie was gone.

Perry lay in bed and listened. . . .

"I'M HUNGRY! I'M HORNY! I'M HUNGRY! I'M HORNY! HERE I AM! HERE I AM! DIE! FOOD! DIE! FOOD! HELP! HELP! OH NO! OH NO! RUN! RUN! RUN! DIE! FOOD! DIE FOOD! OH NO YOU DON'T—OH YES I DO! OH NO! OH YES! OH NO! OH YES! OH! FOOD GOOD! GOOD FOOD! FOOD GOOD! I MAKE SMELL! YOU SMELL? I MAKE SMELL! YOU SMELL!? HELLO! I'M HUNGRY! I'M HORNY! YOU HORNY! YOU HORNY! THIS IS ME! THIS IS MINE! MINE! MINE! MINE! HERE COMES A DANGER! HERE COMES A DANGER! HERE COMES A DANGER!

THIS IS MINE! WATCH IT! WATCH IT! WATCH IT! WATCH IT! WATCH IT!" and so on.

Perry found the animals to be poor conversationalists. Within three days he found their monologues to be unbearable. He reached for his dick, but could not get it hard: the dull calls of the wild distracted him. Perry ran from room to room of his mansion in search of a private place. Finally in the attic, with handkerchiefs stuffed in his ears, he was able to do the deed. And with a billow of smoke the genie appeared.

"Your third and final wish is my command," he said.

"This life of mine sucks. I can't go on any longer. Please, Mr. Genie, take my life away from me. I can't take it any longer. . . . Please kill me."

The genie said that was something he couldn't do. He added, "How do you even know that you are alive anyway?"

"What are you talking about?" said Perry.

"I said, how do you even know if this is really life? I mean, how many men have genies that pop out of their pricks?"

"What are you suggesting? Are you suggesting that I am not even alive? Is that what you are trying to tell me?! Oh!"

The genie said nothing.

"You mean to tell me that all this could be a sham? That, that everything I have ever known. . . . that those egocentric morons out there (the animals). . . that everything, EVERYTHING is a sham? That I have been living some sort of fantasy? Some sort of dead man's fantasy?"

The genie said nothing.

Perry sighed and shook his head. He then walked out of the window.

The genie looked down at the shattered body. Perry was quite dead. And the genie smiled a big, big smile. For his little trick had worked, and now thanks to laws of enchantment, he had Perry's final wish. And being a genie, with lots of experience on his side, he knew exactly what to wish for.

Lost and Found

I'm feeling a little chatty today, so I'll tell you my story—not that it matters—not in the end—but it'll pass the time as we wait. It all happened a long, long time ago. I woke up in the middle of the night and my arm and shoulder ached. I took some aspirin, felt a little better and then went back to sleep. When the alarm went off that morning, I let it go until it shut itself off. I'd go to work, but I'd come in late and to hell with the shower and shave, I told myself. And that's what I did.

I was grungy and sleepy at the job that day. Fortunately, I didn't have any meetings and my phone didn't ring, so all I did was my stupid work that day and was able to keep my mouth shut and not say anything to anybody. Not that I had anyone I wanted to talk to anyway. You see, I've always hated people. "Pee-puhl . . ." even the word sounds hateful and stupid to me. As I took the crowded commuter train home, I was forced to listen to their wretched conversations of violence and stupidity. I hated the people who listened to them too—for engaging and encouraging the idiot talk. All I wanted to do was to get home and be alone finally. To be alone in my own home where I controlled everything and everything was just the way I liked it. And I could be By My Self.

Well, as you probably already figured out, the next day I realized that I was dead.

I was pretty upset at myself for being such a drone for not figuring it out earlier. Nowadays, I know that this is how it works for a lot of folks—and that some retards keep going to their work for decades before they can get the simple fact that they're dead into their fat heads.

How long did it take you to figure it out?

That's great, you're a smarty.

Now where was I? Oh yes . . . well, I was pretty damn happy to find out that I was still me—still myself—and didn't have to a do a damn thing anymore. Didn't have to work, or go shopping, or drink or eat or shit, or do any of that boring human stuff that I had been forced to do all my life. I could just stay at home and be quiet and enjoy my own company. And I did that for a few months and it was paradise for me. Nobody but me. Nothing to do. No people. Just me and the house. Doing my thing the way I liked it. Peace and Quiet.

And then the people came and ruined it . . . the way they always did and still do. All my stuff was taken away and sold or trashed and the house became empty but filled with people: Buyers and Sellers. And then naturally some people moved in and I had to move out. I didn't (like some souls) "haunt" the place, or try to drive the intruders out. I just became homeless for a night or two until I found an empty place to call my own. But, you know, the people would always come and drive me out and I'd have to move on.

Then one day I saw that light you always hear about. It was pretty spectacular and I'd be lying if I told you that I wasn't drawn to it. But then I thought, "I'm not the kind of guy that cues up and stands in lines. I'm not the kind of person who follows the popular herd. If that light is where all the people are going to, then I'm not going!" And I turned my back on that glorious light—that warm sunshine of love and acceptance and all—and I walked away. That wasn't the last time I saw "the light," but I'll tell you about that later.

After a while I decided that I didn't need to live in houses anymore. I really didn't need a roof over my head to protect me from anything anyway, and where there were houses—there were people. And not only the living kind either. The ghosties that I met were just as stupid and obnoxious as they were when they were alive. Vain, stupid, and annoying ghosties! Just like people!

I remember this one time, I was staying in this old, abandoned mansion and there was this other guy living there too. And I thought, well this place is so big that maybe I could just hide away in the eighth bedroom or something and he'll leave me alone. And I told the guy that I just wanted to be alone. And he seemed pretty amenable to the whole idea. But then after a few months, who do you think comes floating into my bedroom with a game of Parcheesi? Right! I play the game with him on the condition that he never does it again and will never come into my room again—ever! But the next day he comes back, and I'm just about to lose it and try to bite his nose off or something, when the ceiling disappears and on comes that fantastic light again. The room fills with all this golden, ethereal light and this time I can hear angelic music, and I say to the guy, "Hey-hey, this is it! This is your big chance!" And I give him a little shove and off he goes. He floats right into the sun on the ceiling and then is gone. And I'm outta there in a flash! I turn and get out of that place as fast as I can go! Then I come back when I figure it's safe. It turned out that I had that place for my ownsome for a couple years . . . until they tore it down.

But yeah, I finally gave up on houses and their ghosties and people and moved to where there are no peoples. I went out into the wilds of the world: the places of ice and cliff where no houses and people are. But you know what? Every now and then somebody does come by—somebody like you or somebody else—but I know what to do about that now. . . .

Don't be scared.

Let me tell you about the time I ended up going into the light. I didn't want to go, you know. But this time the light wouldn't let me escape. It came up on me fast, and when I turned to run, some kind of net caught me and pulled me in. I got pulled to the other side, so to speak. And it was really bright and I was really small and it was another world. I was stuck in this net—like the kind you use to pull fish from fish-tanks—and this big, gigantic monster-thing was holding the net and me and it puts it's truck-sized face up to me and says, "Gotcha!" Then the thing smells me and makes its ugly face even uglier. "Aurgh, I think it's rotten," it says as it makes to toss me away.

"Wait a sec," says another voice, "Don't toss it out. I think I remember this one from way back." The voice belongs to another monster and it walks up next to the other. The thing looks at me closely and says, "Yeah, that's it."

Now I was as scared as I'd ever been—I've never been as scared.

But I say, "Hi" and I wave at 'em. The creatures started laughing and I did too in a nervous way. And after we talked for awhile they sent me back.

The monsters from the other side gave me a job to do. And I'll admit that I haven't done it all that well. I mean I could do better. But I don't think they care how well I do—just as long as I do something. I don't think I'm all that important to them. Thank Whatever.

Now I am going to tell you something real crazy. And when you hear this, you have to consider the source, because I've been up here and down there for over two hundred years now and my mind isn't all that it has been or used to be, if you get my drift. But these monsters told me the secrets about the light—that great light—and what is on the other side and what they do to us. You see they use that light as a kind of a lure. And when we go for that light, like moths to a flame, they scoop us up and sell us at a market to other monsters that like to eat our souls like eggs or something. One of them monsters even asked me "What came first? The human or the soul?" I didn't have an answer. But it's real easy-picking for those guys: just shine a light and fish up the souls when they hit the surface, then sell em to the good folks who likes us scrambled, or hard-boiled, or put into a batter to make a flakey pie. It still makes me laugh to think of it. Our great afterlife in heaven—being someone's breakfast—sitting in an egg cup—having your head scooped off with a spoon. Now that's heaven to me!

You have the time? Great. You see this? What I got in my pocket? When I push the button—watch what happens. . . .

Now there she is! Look at that light! Oh Lordy! Oh Lordy it's beautiful. I feel so calm—so at peace. It's all right now. I was lying. I just can't go. You go. That's it. You go. Good bye. Good bye. Good. . . .

Sucker. Fucking People. Ha! Now where was I? Before I was interrupted? Oh yes. . . .

THE ILLUSTRATED TOM

People always want to know about my tattoos. Do the tattoos have stories behind them? I'd have to say, "Yes." Each tattoo says or marks something important in my life. Some people think of their lives as a novel, or even a book; I think of my life like that too, but my life is more like a picture book. Do tattoos make your life more interesting? Do tattoos create colorful designs that map out a colorful life? Only the sages can answer those bigger questions. But I can show you MY tattoos and tell you the stories of MY interesting life.

Let me take off my shirt. As you can see, I wear an undershirt—but don't worry—there are tattoos under that too!

You see the dragon with the red eyes that covers my left arm and shoulder? Well, the dragon is a very important symbol to the Eastern peoples. The dragon represents good fortune and power and it's scary. I got this tattoo after I got the chance to meet and shake the hand of Steven Segal—the amazing actor/fighter and hero. I was walking down the street when all of a sudden there's Steven Segal coming out of a Quiznos. I stop him and say, "Steven Segal! Let me shake your hand! I've seen all of your movies and. . . ." He backs off and gives me a mean look and says, "It'll cost you twenty bucks to shake my hand." And then he starts to walk away. He must of figured I was a bum, because of the way I was dressed or something. But I was lucky! I had twenty-seven dollars in my wallet. I said, "Here's twenty-seven dollars!" And I gave him the money and I shook his hand! I shook his hand up and down. It was super. It was great! That's why I got the dragon. Good fortune: that's' for having the twenty-seven bucks. Power and scary: that's Steven Segal all over! The bastard! Ha, Ha.

You see the dark-blue hotdog with the smiley face? I got that when I threw my first barbeque. I was living in the Sunset district in a mother-in-law apartment out by the foggy beach. It was almost sunny that day and I had an inspiration! I went to the 7-11 and bought a barbeque set-up and some hotdogs and called a friend. We sat out in the yard on chairs from the kitchen and drank a lot of beer. My friend Steve, who is kind of an artist, gave me the tattoo after we had finished the twelve pack and had started on the Almaden blush wine. He used a pen, a knife, and a potato. And I was so loaded that I only yelled once—and that was because he accidentally set fire to my Hawaiian shirt with his cigarette. We got into a fight a few years ago, Steve and I, over who sang the hit song "Sledgehammer." He thought it was Phil Collins—the ass. I haven't talked to him since—but I still have the artful tattoo!

The Tasmanian Devil on my right bicep is the first tattoo I ever got. I got that one in honor of my graduating Junior High School . . . long story there. . . .

But you see this one, the beautiful lady angel with the machine gun? I got that to commemorate my near death experience on Clear Lake. I was with a bunch of so-called friends staying at a cabin on Clear Lake. They were snorting a lot of Meth and then riding the Jet Ski on the lake. It did look like fun—driving the Jet Ski on Meth. But I'm real afraid of the water because I can't swim. I can't even get my face wet without panicking. Finally at the end of the day, though, I got up enough courage to try the thing. I've driven a motorcycle before, and my friends said it was just like that—except you were on the water. I took a blast of the yellow speed from this chick's fingernail and then got on the Jet Ski and Zoom! Away I went! I didn't do nothing fancy, I just went straight out into the lake. After about a half-hour, when I was just getting the hang of riding the thing (Did you know that there aren't any brakes on a Jet Ski?) there was this sputter and then nothing. I had run out of gas! I was in the middle of the lake just sitting there with no power. The sun had just gone down and there wasn't anyone around me. And that began the longest night of my life. I sat on that Jet Ski in a state of terror all night. I tried to stay awake, because if I fell in the water, I was a goner. I just had to keep sitting! Every once in awhile I would flap my arms and sort of stand a little to keep from going numb. But mostly I just sat there. By morning I must have fallen asleep, because I was awakened by something hitting my head. I was about fifteen feet from shore and some little kids were throwing pinecones at me. I croaked, "Help, help me" and the kids got on their inflatable mattresses, kicked their way into the lake and pushed me to shore. I wanted to give the kids some money for saving me but my wallet was at the cabin, so I just gave em' some cigarettes and shook their little hands. After I found my way back to the cabin, I tore into my so-called friends for not sending help. But they said that they thought I must have found a party on the other side of the lake or something. They were more interested in where the Jet Ski was now—than in how I had nearly died a watery death. I told em all to "F" off and walked out of that place and never saw those guys again.

My near death experience turned my life around. Now I say no to drugs and Jet Skis. And because I'm reasonably sober (I still like to take a beer and do the occasional hit on a doobie) I got a job. I wash and gas Ryder Rental trucks.

Ok, now off with the undershirt! You see the row of skulls and roses that runs down my spine? Those are for the ladies. Every time I get a girlfriend or a girl kisses me, I get a tattoo.

And ladies, I still have room on my lower back for you! Ha-Ha. And of course, there's Mom. The flying snake with the rabbit in its mouth is for my dear, sweet mom.

When I quit my addiction to spicy pork rinds, I got that one on my chest: the Porky Pig with the knife in its head.

And the spider web between my thumb and forefinger was to celebrate getting a DSL hookup.

I could go on and on talking about my tattoos and myself but believe it or not I'm getting kinda shy. You would think that a guy with a hard body covered in pictures would be used to people looking at him. But, like this girl once said about me, I'm kinda like a gorilla in a zoo that sits with its back to you—shy—but with a nice ass.

I'll show you one more. That's Spuds Mackenzie just below my pants here. That crafty ole dog had it going on in those Budweiser commercials in the 80s. You don't see him anymore on TV. But if you know where to look . . . you'll find him. Heh-heh.

THE HATCHING

The henhouse slumbers. Moonlight slips through the wooden slats to slash white the straw littered floor. The henhouse door opens and a small shadow scuttles in. The sounds of fluffed feathers, small clucking sighs and snores greet the intruder. It peers at the chickens with a sidelong glance, and, as silently as a night fog, creeps into the henhouse to rest in an abandoned nest. The chickens sleep and dream. The intruder sits, with eyes the color of smoke and fire; it begins to work.

Mrs. Miriam Darnell hastens to the henhouse, her sneakers stained dark with morning dew. The henhouse door is open, when she knows that she latched it the night before. As she enters, she envisions feathers and blood, or an empty spot on the shelf, as if someone had stolen a prized tea cup from the display case. She expects to see one less chicken. She is surprised to see one more chicken. Instead of 9 chickens she now has 10. A large, healthy, pure white chicken occupies the late Chiquita's nest. This new chicken appears healthy and—and there!—like worshiped pagan stones, white unblemished AAA eggs lay beneath the fanny of feather white. Mrs. Miriam Darnell counts to seven as she touches each blessed egg with a finger. With the glee of finding loose change under a sofa pillow or a forgotten bill in a pocket, she snatches up the eggs and puts them into her basket. She pats this new darling on the head, and, as she moves through the henhouse gathering eggs, she tells her chickens to be nice to this new member of the family. The chicken must have escaped from another farm, from someone careless enough to let it escape. She grabs an extra handful of seed and tosses it to the clucking newcomer, and with this action makes the decision to keep it. She does not realize that throughout the countryside an extra handful of chicken feed is being tossed and the same decision is being made by scores of farmers. . . .

The rising sun paints the kitchen rose-red. On the sink counter are three dozen eggs that have been washed, dried and are ready for market. In a bowl on the kitchen table are seven hardboiled eggs. The eggs have been dyed the pastels of a child's rainbow. Mrs. Miriam Darnell assumes the role of the Easter Bunny, and, followed by the household cat, patronizingly "hides" the eggs throughout the cottage. It is a small thing to delight a child.

Two eyelids jack-in-the-box open to reveal bright, blue eyes. A sleepy, young mind pulls at the wisps of consciousness trying to recall the import of the day. The child has only four years of life experience to draw from. He hears the sounds of something rolling on the hardwood floor and then smacking low against the wall. Peter the cat is playing with something. He has heard this sound before, on a morning, a special morning such as this. . . . The Domino of Cause strikes the Domino of Effect to strike the Domino of Revelation: Peter the cat is playing with an Easter egg.

"It is Easter and the cat is playing with my Easter egg. It is Easter. It is fun. It is an Easter fun day full of surprises and treats!"

Like a circus chimp racing to its tricycle task, the boy runs from his bed to put on his robe and slippers.

Todd Darnell breathlessly pushes open the swinging door to the kitchen as his mother puts the kettle to the stove. She turns and says, "Happy Easter, Todd!" and gives him a hug. She then hands him a toy basket and off he goes: The hunt is on.

A blue, cracked egg is taken away from Peter the cat's unblinking stare. A yellow egg from behind a door. A green egg under a pillow. A purple egg below the bookcase. A golden foil chocolate egg near the closet. Like a mouse in a maze, Todd Darnell bounces from wall to wall, from corner to corner, senses alert—bristling to retrieve. His basket is filling.

Mrs. Miriam Darnell is about to sit down to her coffee when she hears the shrill, happy scream. She knows Todd has found the pot of gold, the Holy Grail, the basket with the green plastic grass filled with jelly beans and the ten-cent balsa-wood airplane. She brings the coffee cup to her lips and sips, but the actual tasting of the coffee is interrupted as Todd bangs into the kitchen, glowing and sweating and smelling of candy.

"Make it for me! Make it for me Mommy!" he demands, as he clumsily pushes the toy airplane to his mother to assemble.

"Yes, yes," she says, "but first, breakfast." She takes the Easter basket and chooses the cracked egg, peels it, washes it, and puts it into a cup.

The boy eats his egg with his special spoon and watches his mother with the miracle hands put together the toy airplane.

The moment the airplane is assembled, the boy drops his empty cup to the table, hops from his chair and smiles with yolk-stained teeth.

"Take it outside and play," is the needless command of Mrs. Miriam Darnell.

Alone in the kitchen, the mother lights a cigarette and drinks her still hot coffee. Her world always quickens and moves at the heightened intensity of her child's when he is around. Now she slows, and sips and smokes. Her mind relaxes and settles and. . . .

And now Mrs. Miriam Darnell stares at an empty coffee cup and a crushed cigarette in an ashtray. She has lost some time again. Her mind slipping away from the here and now to the somewhere and unaware—to the blank place between light and dark. She rouses herself and listens. She hears a rare silence that fills her with fear. Her son always interrupts the quiet with his laughs, cries, demands, shrills, shouts. But it is quiet and something is wrong. "Todd?!" she yells, "Todd?!"

Now she becomes the mouse in the maze, bouncing off walls, moving forward, moving back, calling her child's name—only to hear no reply—heightening her concern, intensifying, senses alert— body bristling in the hunt. She yanks open the henhouse door. She relaxes. Todd is there. But something is perverse and wrong here.

Todd stands, his back to his mother. Before him on a stool sits the new, snow-white chicken. The two are locked together by their eyes, by something else?

"Todd?" she whispers.

The silent boy stands before the chicken with his arms listlessly at his sides, with his legs slightly bent, and his head drooped forward. The chicken clucks low, as if muttering; it does not move its lips.

"Todd?" whispers the mother.

The chicken jerks its head up, then sideways, then blinks and sees. It takes in Mrs. Miriam Darnell. And Mrs. Miriam Darnell is frozen with dread under its assessing glare.

Then with a balloon-pop "Squawk!" the chicken shatters the stillness and flaps its wings.

The boy turns and rushes to his mother and strangles her knees with a hug. He grabs his mother's hand with a strength that she has not felt since the death of her husband and leads her back to the house. "Come, Mommy," says Todd Darnell as he pulls her to the kitchen, "I want you to have an Easter egg with me. They're good. Really good."

The alien chicken sits on the stool in a shaft of sunlight. It clucks and then flies to its nest. A single egg rests on the stool and gleams like wet bone from exposed flesh.

This is how an invasion starts.

MIRROR MAN

The story begins with an alien blob rolling in your still warm bed, gathering all the impressions of your body imprinted in the sheets, as you take your morning shower. The twisting thing becomes an exact duplicate of you. It rises from the bed, and, with arms open, waits for you.

When the shower is over, you walk into the bedroom and find yourself facing another naked self—this is terribly, terribly wrong—and you open your mouth to scream, but a hand covers your mouth. You are pulled to kissing distance and the alien sticks its snaking tongue far up your nose to lick your brain. It tastes you. It savors every flavor of memory, every ingredient and spice of your soul. In this way, the alien learns the recipe of the "who you are" and duplicates it in itself. It becomes—and now totally is—you.

Then the old you is laid to rest on the bed, and the new you gets dressed in the old you's clothes, while you—the old you—watches unable to move. There is some confusion, and in this confusion, the alien forgets to kill you, as it now knows that it has only three minutes to catch the 7:45 bus to get to work on time—to get to the job that is so important to you—and now—the duplicate you.

It grabs your coat, glasses, cigarettes and matches, puts on your hat and turns off the lights and races out, leaving you alone in the dark like the rest of the furniture in a house that is now beginning to feel empty.

The new job is complicated, simple, tedious, and fascinating. Your role in the company is unique and you are a department of one. You are obsessed by the "hows" of the job, while everyone else is only interested in your results. You realize that you are a shy person and that you don't make friends easily. You want to talk about your job but have realized that to do so means to bore others, so you don't. The only person that will listen to you is your supervisor, and she is paid to.

On the home planet there is no such thing as work. One is bred to one's function and one has no need to discuss it. Like a squirrel that gathers nuts, the squirrel does not come home to its mate and say, "Guess what I did at work today?" The squirrel's life is its work, and the distinction of "work" is a false one: You do what you do and that is all.

The alien makes up its mind to kill the human when it gets back "home," and then find the window back to its planet where during deprogramming it will suggest that colonization is inadvisable due to the poisonous culture of the inhabitants. Then the phone rings and grabbing a pen, it takes another order.

The house is cold and dark and you are tired and cranky from the commute home. You turn on the lights and see the human doll drooling and dying on the bed. You should kill it now and get moving, but something stops you. Strange emotions fill your alien mind and you get on the bed, pull the human up, and rest its head on your shoulder.

After a time, you decide to undo the damage you have done to the creature, and after kissing it on the lips, you insert your tongue into its nose. After some tricky tonguing, you feel its body shudder in your arms and then relax.

And then you say, "Today they dropped the Location Number from the Accession, Box and Shipping Code in the ECF. When I called the FRC and asked them how we could fix it in the system, guess what they said?"

You are weak and have the worst headache in your life and are just plain scared, but you find yourself saying, "Well, I bet they weren't helpful. . . ."

"No of course not! In the end, after wasting—Oh God Knows How Much Time—I had to ask Carlos—which is what I should have done in the first place—and he told me that just by selecting 'change location' in the ECF and then hitting 'reference select,' I could access 'location' and scroll down to the code number that was dropped when they deleted the DMA!"

"Oh for Christ's sake was that all?

"Of course! But you know what it's like trying to get. . . ."

" Oh, I know—I know!"

"And then this morning. . . ."

You chatter and chirble like two parakeets in a cage as dusk turns to dark and thoughts finally turn to dinner.

* * *

Over a year passes and still he has not returned to his home planet. The transfer was too complete. The duplication too perfect. He is happy with the new life he has with his friend and job.

He is happy with the new crazy life. He alternates work days with his other self and has more time to relax now. He doesn't feel lonely anymore and there is someone who is always interested in hearing about work. Also they share tastes in music, movies, books—everything!

There is always someone to come home to.

They wish that they could go out together, but preferring not to cause a scene, just enjoy their time together at home. In some ways, they are the perfect couple.

The story ends with this bit of dialogue and action. . . .

"I'm not boring you—am I?"

" No! Never! Go on!"

" I gotta say first, I'm so happy that you came into my life."

"Oh, me too. We make a good team."

"We make a good team."

That night they make love for the first time.

DUNCAN'S DIAGNOSIS

A Guide To Medical Self Care

Space Poisoning: Sylyhian Parasites

What most people call space poisoning is actually quite rare. In order to have true space poisoning, one must have diarrhea accompanied by a high fever and acute pain in the lower abdomen, followed by severe constipation and painful bloating. Bloodshot eyes and a stiff neck must also be prevalent for the diagnosis of space poisoning. If you are not experiencing diarrhea with a high fever accompanied by bloodshot eyes and a stiff neck see page 257 for Food Poisoning and Diarrhea.

Space poisoning is a bacterial infection caused by eating shrimp, and, although the symptoms of discomfort are extreme, the condition passes within a week and seldom causes permanent injury. Some intestinal bleeding may occur and hemorrhoids are a common byproduct of the infection. There is no known remedy for the condition but patience.

When infected by space poisoning you are actually becoming part of the Sylyhian Parasite's reproductive cycle. The Sylyhian Parasite injects its eggs into shrimp in the hopes that the infected shrimp will be netted and eaten by man. Once inside its human host, the eggs hatch and lock onto the intestinal wall, drawing nutrients until the parasites are fully formed. The maturation process takes six to seven days. Then the young parasites are excreted and make their way through the sewer systems back to the sea. How the parasites arrived on our planet is unknown. However, after the first outbreaks of the infection in the late 2040s, improved shrimp processing techniques and waste disposal methods have all but eradicated the disease in the First and Second Worlds.

Treatment

As in any case where diarrhea is present there is a risk of dehydration. Sip clear fluids, or put ice under the tongue if water cannot be tolerated. The bouts of diarrhea are short and should pass within a day. It is important not to use Pepto Bismo, or other over-the-counter, anti-diarrhea medications that contain silicates which solidify the stool and constipate. The body's quick diarrhea reaction naturally flushes many of the parasite eggs from the body before they hatch and constipating medications can exacerbate the infection. Let the diarrhea do its work.

Use buffered aspirin or accetaphmine to reduce the fever and stiffness in the neck. Other forms of pain-killing and fever-reducing drugs may cause stomach bleeding and the parasites will move to the ruptured area to feed.

During the secondary phase of the infection, bloating and constipation occur, as well as a loss of appetite. It is important to eat during the illness, as the parasites do deplete the body of many important minerals and red blood cells. Eat easily digested foods such as eggs, organ meats, applesauce, oatmeal, and Jell-O. Avoid high fat foods and hard cheeses. Drink plenty of fluids, especially grape juice, which is high in carbohydrates and gives quick energy.

Some find relief from the discomfort of bloating by placing hot towels on the stomach area, or by lying in a warm bath with the legs raised.

Constipation sets in on the second or third day; bowel movements become completely impossible during the last three days of the infection. Contrary to common health practices, high fiber and fiber supplements such as psyllium should not be taken during the final days of this illness. The parasites grow much quicker than any earth organism and when excreted will be five to seven inches long with the diameter of a tennis ball. The infected person will have to pass up to four of the organisms and the strain to the bowel sac is already pushed to the limit without added fiber bulk.

It is in the best interests for the parasites not to have the bowel burst, so on the sixth day, they reduce their numbers. The strange gurgling sounds and violent movements that are felt in the lower abdomen are the result of the larger parasites conquering and devouring their weaker siblings. Occasionally, the battles become fierce and discomfort can be extreme, but this is a signal that the infection is nearly over.

After a week, when the parasites are ready to leave, the body's voiding mechanisms are triggered and elimination will finally occur. Because of the size and volume of the foreign matter, elimination may be painful, but most people feel only a sense of profound relief at the end of the process. Check the stools to see if they are darkened as that is a sign of internal bleeding. The creatures themselves are an emerald green.

It is important not to attempt to kill the parasites as they lay in the bowl, as their skin, when broken, emits a gas that can irritate the eyes and throat. Be comforted in the knowledge that they will die. The parasites have an extremely short lifespan of just fourteen days—they will die soon.

As stated earlier, because of modern sewage treatment and shrimp processing techniques this bacterial infection by the Sylyhian Parasite is extremely rare.

Time Travelers

Richard Paintfield lay in his bed in the wardroom and watched his chest rise and fall with each labored breath. He struggled to roll onto his side, spitting out a curse at his failed body, and assumed the fetal position.

Richard Paintfield was born in 1960. He was now 109 years old—the oldest man on the West Coast—and tomorrow was his birthday.

He yelled, "Hey do you wanna' play a game of racquetball?" to his partner, Troy Monatage, who occupied the cot to his left, but Troy didn't respond. Troy wasn't talking that day. Richard didn't mind—he found himself slowly buried in warm sand, feeling the sand begin to fill him with sleep.

Tomorrow, or was it today, the press would come to help him celebrate his birthday, to ask him his secret of longevity. "Treat each day as a gift. Like a gift that you want to return because it's the wrong size." He chuckled a bit at his statement. The gag didn't make that much sense. "Not much sense," he muttered aloud as sleep pushed its way in. "Not much sense, that's the gist of it," he thought.

Then Richard Paintfield fell away, bullied into submission by sleep . . . to awake in another world. . . .

The little alien child sidled up to its father and watched him slice open the top of Richard Paintfield's head. The father sensed the alert and energetic presence of his child's mind and waited for it to think-speak its question.

"What is it that they call themselves? A human being?"

"Yes, that's right," thought-said the father, as it extracted the human brain.

"What are you doing?"

"We were very fortunate to procure this old creature. Its brain will allow us to observe 110 years of human history. This brain, although primitive, is still quite a marvel. It holds every scrap of sensory input recorded during the creature's lifetime, information that we can review and learn from . . . once properly prepared that is," added the alien dad.

It then began to work like a sushi chef, as it rapidly and expertly sliced up the brain, keeping the choice parts and pushing the excess aside. . . .

"This portion contains the animal's sex, hunger, and sleep drives . . . we won't be needing that. The visual sensory organs— no. And this here . . . this here—this is a bit tricky—this contains the creature's consciousness, its personality, behavior patterns, memories, knowledge, etc. But, we won't be needing that. What we want is just the pure recorded data, unencumbered by defects of the alien personality. This is what we want."

The alien child touched its father and said, "What are you going to do with it . . . the consciousness part? Just throw it away?"

The father, proud of his precocious child's sense of economy, replied, "Why, do you want it?"

"Oh please father!" cried the child's mind.

The larger alien looked down upon its shuffling child and thought-said, "These creatures are very primitive, yet noble in their way. There are even those who say that we are evolutionarily linked. And yes, yes, we shall see what we can do. . . ."

The alien child excitedly bounced on its tail with glee.

When Richard Paintfield awoke, he instantly realized something was terribly wrong. He could not speak or move his body. He could see, but what he could see didn't make any sense. He was in an enormous room with walls that shifted from one primary color to the next, and what looked like real planets and comets floated in a black sea above him. Richard figured either he had had a stroke, or was still asleep, or perhaps had been drugged, or was in heaven—

dead. Then he began to scream. A giant monster lifted him up to its horrendous face and laughed into his own. He could not stop screaming for a long time. . . .

But life goes on . . . and Richard Paintfield accepted his new role in life. Richard Paintfield, in his very long life, had learned to roll with the punches. He had seen his new body: the stitched smile, the cartoonish eyes, the exaggerated mockery of human form, the permanent clothing painted to his fabric flesh. He had been given a dress to wear and long hair. (Since the alien was female, perhaps they thought that he should be too.) He had some kind of battery in his back that kept the lights on in his head. Yet, he could still sleep and dream just about whenever he wanted to. He was a doll . . . and he belonged to a child—an alien child—that could read his thoughts, and wanted to play with him, and was just as intelligent as he was, if not more so.

Yes, he was Richard Paintfield . . . and he was a doll. An alien girl-child named Carlona owned him. She understood his language and was interested in him. He told her stories and sang for her. And together they became friends in an intimate, platonic fashion. He thought of her as a good, clever girl—albeit alien. And she thought of him as her strange, funny dolly-child from another world. And Richard rolled with the punches and became somewhat content in his new life.

* * *

Time moved differently for Richard the Doll in his new world: What would have been a month on Earth seemed to be only a day. And after a few "days" Carlona noticed a change in Richard.

"What's wrong, Topper?" (The name that she gave him and that he accepted.)

"Oh, I don't know. I'm not feeling myself today—or maybe—that's just it—maybe I am. I don't know. I think I miss . . . oh, what's the use, there's nothing you can do about it."

Carlona picked him up and held him. "Let's not be so sure," she thought-said. "Tell me—what's on you're mind?"

"Well I miss my real body," thought back Richard the Doll, "I miss breathing and walking and being a human being with other human beings. I miss everything. That's it. I miss it all. I miss it all the fucking all."

Carlona was quiet for a moment and thoughtful. She then said, "Well, there's not much I can do about the body, but I have an idea."

He was carried to a darkened room and placed upright on a table. Then suddenly the room vanished and he found himself in a different world. He was back on earth, it seemed, viewing a living room that looked familiar. He saw the tiny human hands of a baby pick up a Cheerios and raise it until the fingers disappeared. He was looking at the room from an infant's perspective. There was a black-and-white television before him and some dancing puppets on it, and then the screen abruptly changed. An anchorman appeared on the TV. The point of view moved erratically about the room, then turned up and back to reveal a young woman. Richard then understood. He saw his own mother—so young—so beautiful—so alive—and she was crying. He understood now that he was viewing his own life, seeing something that had happened over a hundred years ago—and he was overwhelmed. As he stared at his young mother, he felt the hopeless enormity of his life—of his past, of his joys and loves, of his every forgotten and remembered memory of being—and it all fell on him at once. And as he stared at his crying mother—he began to cry too.

Carlona, sensing his pain, picked him up and squeezed him. "Don't cry Topper! Don't cry! You're my favorite doll. My favorite! You're my favorite doll and I'll never let anything bad happen to you," and she hugged and kissed him.

And from behind his stitched smile, Richard smiled and felt the child's love. "This is the day President Kennedy was shot," he thought-said. "This is one of my first memories."

"What's a president?"

"Oh, a president is. . . ."

Looking For Love

When Don Teddy first walked into the examination room, I had no idea of the absolute marvels he held. He was a short, sixty-year-old man with a soft, cheerful face and flabby body. The only slightly exceptional thing about Don was that he was completely hairless and didn't seem to mind the testing. The man was docile and compliant to my every request and received the colonoscopic exam without a trace of fear or discomfort. As I pressed the scope into his anus, I recall he blinked like a toad and sighed.

Don Teddy had been referred to me by his primary physician, Dr. Richard Fell. It was a routine exam. Don's family had a history of cancer. I was searching for abnormal polyps, or inflammations or growths. There had been some blood in his stool some weeks ago, but that probably was because of constipation due to PSA (Patient Sample Anxiety), a common occurrence.

For the first three minutes the exam went normally. The scope inched forward—the tissue tunnel was lit and explored—the scope inched forward again. No abnormalities, just a good clean rectum and bowel. But when I reached the sigmoid colon something strange and wonderful happened! First there was a flash of white light, then a shuddering shake of vision, and then the colon disappeared, and . . . and a fantastic vista fell before me. I saw the manicured lawn of a British country manor. The sky was blue and dotted with cloud. And tall statues of Greek gods lined a gravel path leading to an ancient estate on top of a hill. . . .

I jerked my head back and away. Surely I was hallucinating! I looked again—nothing had changed—the marvelous English countryside still lay before me. However, this time I saw . . . fairies. Three fairies to be exact. They flew on wings translucent and sparkling. They were grand and strong with bodies slender and ageless. Two fairies I took to be the king and queen—for although they were nude—they wore crowns. The third, I took to be their daughter. She was adult, my age I thought, and was the most beautiful thing I had ever seen in my life.

The fairies seemed to notice my spying eye for they flew right up to me. Up close it was hard not to gasp in awe at their magnificent, perfectly formed bodies. I realized that, although naked, they wore eyeliner and artful makeup. The King winked. The Queen smiled. The Princess (for what else could she be?) threw me a bouquet of butterflies. She approached me until her face filled my sphere of vision. Her eyes widened and took me in totally. It was an honest look of appraisal, and, because of her slight smile, approval—I hoped! Then her full lips puckered and encompassed all. I fell back away as I felt her loving kiss.

Now before me lay a sixty-year-old man lying prone on a table with his white ass in the air. He turned his head toward me and said, "See anything Doc?"

I shook my head "No" and looked back into the scope: the fairies and their world had vanished.

I quickly and professionally finished the exam. Don Teddy was in picture perfect health. I told him to dress, told him the good news and sent him on his way.

Later that night, I called Dr. Fell to schedule another appointment with his patient. I told him that I had seen some growth on a polyp. I lied.

I had to look into Don Teddy's fantastic rectum again—I had to!

* * *

Three days later, I had him in my office. Don Teddy good-naturedly asked me why I hadn't told him that I had seen growths on his first visit. He told me he was a little worried. I told him that I wasn't really sure if there was anything really wrong, but that I might have seen something that upon reflection needed more investigation, but not to worry, and that he should drop his pants and prepare himself.

Minutes later, I was in him and searching!

I found it again: the English countryside, the statues...and her.

The Princess had been waiting for me. She seemed so happy to see me. And I, without pretense or anxiety or judgment, felt so happy to see her. We could communicate just by sharing thoughts . . . and she was so intelligent and funny and wise. She introduced me to her pretty, pink panda named "Mandy" that she keeps as a pet. And I asked her about her world and told her of mine. We must have talked for hours, until the complacent Don Teddy finally broke our reverie with a loud grunt of discomfort, and a "Hey hello, are you done back there yet?"

She kissed me and flew away. And I went back to my office and my world.

As I poured my second drink in my quiet apartment, I considered that I might be going mad. I had looked into the bodies of thousands upon thousands of patients and had never experienced "fairy worlds." I had seen nothing more unusual than polyps or the occasional misplaced anal toy. But I wanted this mad world of enchanted gardens and fairies to be true. I didn't seem to care if Don Teddy's colon was the path to madness. I just wanted my Fairy—my new Fairy—my new Fairy Love.

I thought of my past romantic relationships: my train wrecks, my slow-leaking failures, my youthful crushes—crushed. Long ago I had given up on love. I just didn't have it in me anymore. But here was someone I could love. I did love. I did love. I did love my Fairy Princess. Could it be because she was unattainable that I loved her so?

No, we would be together. We would have to be! She could do it. I could do it too. "Fairies are magic, you know," I thought as I sipped my drink.

The following Tuesday, Don Teddy missed his appointment. I called Don Teddy and he refused to speak to me. I called Dr. Fell's office and insisted upon speaking to him, "Now." When he finally got on the line, he told me that Don Teddy had received a second opinion, that there was nothing wrong, that I was either incompetent or insane, and that I would never get another referral again, no matter what the HMO said.

I stood in my office listening to the dial tone and slowly began to panic. I had to find my fairy world. I hadn't seen it in any other body besides Don Teddy's. I needed that fat fool's body! Perhaps I could sneak into his house, overcome him, plug the scope into his. . . . No, the scope wasn't portable. And . . . and I wasn't capable of anal rape no matter what my needs were. No, there had to be another way.

And then a wild, wonderful idea came to me. It was a leap of faith, A Great Hope: Why not look inside myself? My heart raced and my hands trembled as I dropped my pants and lubed the tube. I shut my eyes and said a quick, simple prayer, "Please God. Please. Please." I stuck the scope into my ass.

I searched and searched and found it! She was there, beautiful, naked, and mine. I told her that I wanted to give up my world—to move into hers—to be with her always. I told her that I loved her and that I hoped she loved me. I asked her as a fairy to use her magic. Could it be done? Could she bring me to her world?

She laughed happily, kissed me, and said, "All you had to do was ask." She then closed her eyes and raised her arms.

I felt as if I were a child being thrown into the air and caught, thrown into the air and caught, thrown into the air and. . . .

And then I landed onto the English countryside and stood upon the lawn beside my Fairy—my Fairy Love.

We walked along the path, past the Greek statues and into the ancient manor. And there I've been ever since. . . .

My Fairy and I are very happy and very much in love. My Fairy says that in order to love, you must first look inside yourself and find the love—the love of yourself—before you can give and receive it. I think she is right, and that in some ways, my story is a literal representation of the fact. But who knew that I would find my love, first in the ass of another man, and then in my own, and finally in the heart of another.

LIKE YESTERDAY

She loved her dying husband. She helped him to bed, settled him upright, and, reading from the carton, began to prepare the drug.

He watched her silently as she moved about the familiar room and felt a little afraid. The drug was relatively new and the list of side-effects was a malady train of misery that would take a speed-talking auctioneer three full minutes to complete. "Like Yesterday" was the cute name for the polysyllabic, psychotropic type drug. He was afraid of the stuff because it screwed with your head. He was born at the tail-end of the Baby Boom and was not a stranger to mind altering drugs like Acid and 'Shrooms, but that hallucinogenic tripping-in-the-woods phase of his life ended fifty years ago and his mental faculties were all that he had—as they were. But the authority figure that was The Doctor had prescribed the drug to help his mental state, which he admitted was lousy to the point of suicidal. This drug had been proved effective in the psychological treatment of the sad elderly who faced chronic illness; it gave them a mental boost, a shot in the arm of will power, a swift kick in the ass of survival.

"What the hell," he thought as he took the offered sedative from his wife and took a sip, "Some folks take this stuff recreationally. Who knows? It could be fun." He said out-loud to his wife, however, somewhat dramatically, "I love you," as she placed the dermal patch to his forehead.

* * *

She watched her sleeping husband and steeled herself for the upcoming morn. When he would awaken, fifty years of memory and experience would be suppressed by the drug, leaving him at the same mental state that he was when he was a teenager. And that "Teen" would not know her, would be confused and disoriented, and it would be her job to help him through that day—his one day of existence—that would end with sleep. Her husband (when he returned to her) would have the fresh, concise memory of his youth—not episodic and clouded by age and ego, oh no—crystalline and sharp memories of who he was. Strong memories to be renewed by and recalled . . . like yesterday.

"I know I am going to love that boy," she thought. And then she began to worry.

* * *

Dean Crosby awoke in a strange bed and into an even stranger world. There was this freaky old lady in his room that wanted to know all these things about him and said crazy stuff about this not being 1978, but being the future (2028!) and that he was himself in the future and that he was old and dying-n-shit. And all he wanted to do was get the hell out of there and get home. Mom would be really pissed about his not coming home last night, and speaking of pisses, he had to like a race horse. Then the mirror in the bathroom made him scream and almost have a fuckin' heart attack. And he had to sit down on the edge of the bed and catch his breath and really listen to this crazy old bag who said she was his wife. It was a fucking nightmare.

Dean got overwhelmed, and, although it was embarrassing, he cried for awhile—it was just too much. But she told him to think of it all like some big, crazy dream that would be over sooner than you thought, and that when he woke up, like in *A Connecticut Yankee in King Arthur's Court*, he would be back in his own time. Dean knew that that wasn't how *A Connecticut Yankee in King Arthur's Court* really ended—Merlin poisoned the fucking guy first—but he kept his mouth shut and figured that this woman was probably right. And besides, what could he really do? Wasn't he trapped inside an old fucked-up body?

"Just try and let it ride," he thought, like he did on that acid trip. With the right attitude, he'd get through it, maybe have some fun or learn something and then have something to tell the guys later. . . .

* * *

He was shocked at the price of a cup of coffee and was very

disappointed when he couldn't get a cigarette. He walked so much faster than normal and seemed somehow taller. She noticed that his eyes moved quickly from one object to the next. And he seemed so very anxious and nervous and high-strung. She remembered that Dean had not had his first sexual encounter until he was nineteen and that he was still a virgin. She toyed with the possibility of trying to seduce him, thereby being his first, but upon a moments reflection, dropped the idea as being distasteful. His vocabulary was very salty and he overused certain words to the point of exhaustion. He was very bright and curious about his new world of the future. He also found their plight amusing in a smug manner and had that removed arrogance and disdain of the teenager for the adult world.

The heated, angry planet in its death throes, the mass extinction of species, the fall of the First World to the Third World, the global depression, the wars, the rise of crime and the new vigilantism—all held less interest to him than the latest gimmick technology and . . . girls. She almost slapped him for ogling a sexpot siren in her teens! He even had an erection, she noted (something to bring up with old Dean later, she thought).

When asked, she skirted the issue of his parents, saying that they had moved to a retirement home in the country and were doing fine; he seemed all too willing to accept this, as if the realties of the present were just one big weird joke. He treated his body as an elaborate costume, even at one point playing up his aging fragility as if it were a gag. He did have her Dean's sense of humor and she liked him. But she had never related to children very well and she could tell that he was becoming bored with her. He asked to see the city. And she treated him like a visiting relative and gave him the tour.

* * *

Back at the apartment, Dean finished his dinner and began to get a little freaked out. That old lady was nice enough, and it certainly seemed like she liked him, but he was beginning to get creeped-out by her somehow. She kept staring at him, and Christ, he wasn't *that* interesting! Also this wasn't like any kind of trip or dream that he had ever had. And it wasn't ending! The body he was in hurt, and it had to go to the bathroom all the fucking time, and it weighed a ton.

Now she wanted to know if he wanted to go to bed, "Alone . . . don't worry."

Dean got up and started for the door, saying, "Hey I'm just going to go out for a bit. I'm going to see some friends, that's all. I'll be back. Don't worry."

She said that's all right, but why not have a drink and a smoke before leaving? She had some good wine and a smoke hidden away someplace . . . and he agreed; it seemed so adult having a drink and a smoke with a woman after dinner-n-shit, and then afterwards he'd run.

The wine tasted great—the second glass even better—the third tasted kinda funky. And then something started to happen to him. He began to feel sluggish and tired and a little weak. And it all came down—this wasn't a fuckin dream or drug trip—this was real—and what that old woman had said was true. And now she wanted her old man back! "And if he comes back, where will I go?" he thought.

Dean got up and swayed toward the door. The old woman blocked the door. He smiled as he grabbed her and threw her aside. But she grabbed him from behind and he felt her strength. And suddenly he was weak. And the next thing he knew he was on the floor. And she was on top of him—crying all kinds of crazy love things.

He almost pitied her and thought for a moment of giving up and letting sleep overcome him and letting the other Dean back in. He had toyed with suicide before; it was just a game anyway. But the fear locked in, for if he fell asleep where would he go? Would he go back into the nothing? The nothing that was before he was born? Would he cease to exist? Would he die?

"No!" he shrieked as he struggled. The bitch weighed a ton and he couldn't get away. "No . . . I DON'T WANT TO FUCKING DIE!" he screamed, and then "Oh god . . . oh god!"

And then sleep began to flood-fill him . . . or was it death?

Mark Romyn

Mark Romyn is an actor, playwright and comedian. Born and raised in San Francisco, he was educated by the city's public schools and by San Francisco State University. He has worked as a barista, bartender, and file clerk. Currently he is employed at the United States District Court as a records clerk. He has written countless short stories, many published in local zines and online magazines. He performs at EXIT Theatre's Thursday Night Combo, the San Francisco variety show that he has hosted since 2004.

His novella, published in 1996, "Flyscraper," is available through Permeable Press. His new apocalyptic novella, "Tired of Waiting," will be published soon by EXIT Press.

EXIT Press

EXIT Press is the publishing division of EXIT Theatre, a San Francisco theater company founded in 1983. Published books include *Ten Plays* by Mark Jackson, *Snakes of Kampuchea* by Mark Knego, and *Woyzeck, Pelleas and Melisande, Ubu Roi* translated by Rob Melrose. Coming soon *Songs of Hestia: Five Plays from the 2010 San Francisco Olympians Festival.*

Made in the USA
Las Vegas, NV
02 May 2024

89429514R00067